# starting out

je rowney

This book is also available as an eBook, and can be read for free as part of a Kindle Unlimited subscription.

Scan this page with your Smart Phone camera to access the eBook.

Also by this author

Charcoal
The Derelict Life of Evangeline Dawson
Ghosted
I Can't Sleep
The Woman in the Woods

THE LESSONS OF A STUDENT MIDWIFE SERIES:

Life Lessons
Love Lessons
Lessons Learned

The On Call Midwife at Christmas

## Chapter One

With Zoe sitting across the table from me in our favourite coffee shop, this could be any Monday afternoon. She has her mocha – extra hot, extra shot – and I have my latte. Anyone that's seen us here, week-in week-out over the past three years, would think that nothing has changed at all.

They would be wrong.

Everything has changed, or at least everything is changing.

I was staying in Zoe and her fiancé Luke's new place from when we moved out of our student house two weeks ago up until yesterday. Then the pair of them, my best friends, helped me to move my small collection of belongings across the small town we live in, into my new home.

Three years at uni, three years of living together, and now it's just me, alone in a one-bedroom flat.

And there are more changes to come.

"Did you sleep alright after we left?" Zoe asks.

She's got her flame red hair tied back in her *I'm-a-professional-teacher-now* ponytail, and it bobs forward, dangerously close to the foam on her latte as she leans towards me. She started her new job last week, fresh out of teacher training and straight into a great job in a high school five minutes from where she lives. She worked hard, got her first-class degree and she deserves every ounce of success.

Did I sleep alright? I don't want her to worry about me, I never want her to worry about me, so instead of telling her that I went to bed at ten, but ended up lying awake, looking at the ceiling for two hours before giving up and taking the duvet through to my new sofa in my new living room and lounging in front of my new television. Apart from the duvet, of course none of the things are actually new. They are all just new to me. Second-hand new, that sums up my life right now.

I shrug and make an indistinct grunting noise in response.

"You're going to get used to it so quickly, Vi," she says. "You'll wonder how you ever put up with living with us for so long once you're settled in."

It was inevitable really that once we left our student accommodation Zoe would move in with Luke. Her fiancé. I haven't even had time to get used to that change, never mind adjust to renting a flat on my own. They've been engaged for two months, but they're already planning the wedding. It's September now, and they're aiming to get married in December. So soon, but somehow it seems so right.

No, she's not pregnant. It's nothing like that. They are hopelessly, completely in love though. Two years together and nothing but good times. I can only hope that one day I find something similar. For now though, I live vicariously through Zoe's happiness. She's been my best friend since we were toddling around at nursery and I've never seen her as happy as she is now.

"Living with you and Luke was the best," I say. Before she can cut in and apologise for moving on with her life, I start my next sentence. "I know you needed to get a place together. That's what couples do, isn't it?"

"Oh Violet, I –"

I shake my head. The last thing I want is to make my best friend feel bad because she has an amazing, happy relationship and I am a sad old spinster. I'm twenty-one, there's plenty of time, I'm sure. I'm not sad, I'm not very old, and right now I don't particularly care whether I end up as a spinster or not. I've not had much luck in relationships so far, but right now I have something else to focus on. Something much more important than any man. Especially Him.

"Hey," Zoe says, snapping my attention back towards her. "You're not thinking about him, are you?"

Him. It's been six months, but something about That Guy is still niggling away at me. Not because I have residual feelings for him; I don't. He made me feel wonderful, and then he stripped that away from me and left me feeling, well pretty worthless.

"No point really, is there?" I jab my fork into the remains of the Bakewell slice on the plate in front of me, and stuff it into my mouth.

"No," she says. "There isn't." Zoe sighs and reaches out to put her hand onto mine. "This is a time for new beginnings. For both of us. You're in your new flat, we're both starting out in our *careers*." She says that last word in a mock-posh accent, letting go of me to raise her fingers in mock quotation marks. It does all sound very grown up, but I suppose that's what we are now.

"To be honest, I'm terrified," I tell her. My eyes meet hers, searching for reassurance.

"Of what? The flat? Starting work?"

"I meant work, but yes, I guess I'm terrified of living on my own and having to act like an adult."

Even though my face is deadpan, Zoe grins.

"Nobody said that we have to act like adults," she says, dipping the end of her spoon into her mocha and flicking foam at me.

"Oi!" My protest must appear very feeble seeing as I can't stop myself from laughing. I dab the chocolatey froth off my nose and reach out to tickle her beneath her ribs. I know that's her most vulnerable area, and she knows very well that I know. She crunches her body to avoid my fingers, and I almost fall off my chair trying to gain purchase.

"Okay, okay," she laughs. "Truce?"

"For now," I smile.

Twenty-one years old, a qualified midwife, but still an immature idiot. I'll take it.

When I get home after my mate date I walk straight through the living room, only pausing to throw my coat onto the back of the bottle-green sofa. I have plans for tonight. I head straight for the bathroom, flick on the taps and pour a generous dollop of sweet-scented bath cream into the tub. Tomorrow is my first shift as a newly qualified midwife, so tonight's plan is that I am going to do absolutely nothing. Long bath, microwaved junk food and trashy television.

My flat isn't all that bad. In fact, it's pretty great. I say that as someone who spent the first eighteen years of her life living at home, and the past three co-habiting with her best friend in a student residence. Our old place, Tangiers Court, never felt like a student house though. It was home. Zoe and I made it our own, and leaving it behind was a sombre affair. We had a moving out party – just the three of us: me, Zoe, and Luke – and I know that I'll never forget my time there and everything I learned. That was also where I met That Guy, but, as I told Zoe, there's no point thinking about him.

The place that I moved into over the weekend, with the help of Zoe and Luke, is a one-bedroomed flat above a deli-style café. I haven't had chance to visit '*Bon Appétit*' as it's called. Zoe and I may have lived in Cranbourne for the past three years, but we are loyal to *Coffee Express* and our regular Monday meetups always happen there. My cosy (estate agent speak for *small*) living room looks out over a fairly quiet road. It's not quite town centre, but not quite part of the main residential area of Cranbourne: close to the bus route to work, and convenient for the shops. My first night here, last night, was peaceful enough, but then again it was a Sunday. Fingers crossed it stays that way.

Tomorrow is my first shift as a newly qualified midwife. To be honest, terrified doesn't even begin to explain how I feel, but I don't want Zoe stressing about me. She has enough to deal with planning her wedding, and settling into her own new job and new home. I've spent the last three years training for this career. Straight out of college and into a direct-entry midwifery course, no prior nursing training, just the desire, the deep, unrelenting desire to be a midwife, to support women and help them to have the best experience of pregnancy, birth, and the postnatal period that they can. If you ask any aspiring midwife why she wants to enter a profession with unsociable hours and long shifts, a profession that requires a deep emotional investment, they will probably tell you the same thing: I want to make a difference. The thing is, to do that you have to give your heart and soul. You have to put everything you have into everything you do. There's no blagging it, no faking it. Midwifery takes a strong, determined, resolute personality. I'd like to say that I have that, but some days, like today, I doubt myself. I doubt my skills, I doubt my knowledge, I doubt myself.

My training has made me a stronger person, but I have suffered from anxiety and self-doubt for almost ten years now. I haven't managed to overcome them completely; I'm starting to wonder if I've even begun to overcome them at all. I got through my training, but was it a fluke? Do I really deserve the degree certificate and the job it has helped me to land in the hospital in which I trained?

All I know is that I have the rest of this evening alone in my flat to overthink and worry, worry, worry about taking my first steps onto the ward as a newly qualified midwife.

Actually, today was the official start date of my new role, but like most staff members the first day was spent undertaking my Trust Induction. Imagine a series of welcome chats, mini-seminars and short ice-breaker sessions wrapped around a buffet lunch with limp sandwiches and warm lettuce. You've got it. Induction is one of the many things that I have to get signed off as part of my preceptorship program. During the next twelve months I'll receive support to adapt to becoming a qualified, fully functioning member of staff, and in turn I'll have to evidence that I am competent and capable.

Making the transition from student midwife to newly qualified practitioner isn't as straightforward as you might think. Yes, I completed my course, scraping through with a lower second-class degree, and more importantly gaining those two letters after my name that mean that I am now Violet Cobham RM.

RM. Registered Midwife.

Technically, anyway. On paper I've been signed off as fit and ready for practice. To start working as a midwife on the ward, I need my PIN – the number that is allocated to all professionals that are registered with the Nursing and Midwifery Council. I'm starting off as a supernumerary staff member – not counted in the numbers but expected to work all the same. It could take a couple of weeks for my PIN to come through, so I'll use the time to find my feet. I expect I'll find them in much the way a newborn deer would find theirs – by wobbling a little and falling over a few times. I've been allocated a mentor, and the Trust has an awesome preceptorship programme, but starting out as a qualified midwife is the most exciting and most nail-bitingly scary experience of my life.

As I lower myself into the steamy bubble bath I try to let these thoughts float from my mind. I let my body slide beneath the surface, immersing every part in the warm, comforting water.

"This is a time for new beginnings," Zoe said.

This is everything I ever wanted. This is everything I have worked for.

I can't let my anxiety get the better of me now. I have to focus, and I have to be strong. I want to make a difference. I want to make a difference for myself too.

I'm not sure if I am ready, but I can do this.

Can't I?

## Chapter Two

Despite the dread-laden thoughts that filled my mind as I lay down for the second night in my new home, I managed to sleep. I'm awake before my alarm beeps at six-thirty, and filled with a mix of excitement and terror. My first day as a newly qualified midwife is an early shift on the postnatal ward. Although my favourite place to be in the maternity unit is delivery suite, I was rather relieved that I wasn't going to be starting out there. I've had my own allocations of women to care for on the postnatal ward before, as a student, and I feel almost confident that I will be able to do everything I need to without asking for help too often.

There's no lounging in bed this morning. I have time to take it easy, but my feet are on the floor, sinking into my new shaggy rug almost as soon as I've silenced the beeping. I want the excitement to take over. I can't let my mind fixate on the fear. I have to focus on this: I made it. I am a midwife. I did it.

I grab breakfast, making a mental note to pick up more milk, and head back through to my room to get dressed.

My uniform is hanging in my wardrobe, or at least one of the three sets of navy tops and bottoms that I collected from the unit. It will have to stay there a while longer. While I'm waiting for my PIN,

I have to wear a pale blue top instead. It's the same as the maternity support workers wear, which is fitting, as I'll basically be carrying out the same role as them for however long it is until my PIN comes through. Out with the student lilac and in with the halfway-house sky blue. It still feels like a rite of passage, pulling the tunic over my head for the first time and looking into the huge oval mirror on my dressing table. Not that I never thought I would make it this far or anything, but, well, I can't believe that I've actually done it. I qualified. My lilac days are behind me.

I stop for a few moments, looking at my reflection in wide-eyed disbelief. I really did it. I'm really doing it. I choke back a sob, and wipe frantically at my eyes, trying to stop myself from crying. The last thing I need is to turn up late because I have to redo my make-up. I only ever wear simple mascara and foundation really, but arriving at work on the first day looking like a startled panda isn't going to be a great image.

Everyone already knows me, of course. That's one of the massive benefits of getting my first midwifery job in the hospital that I trained at. St. Jude's is local, friendly, and I already feel an intimate connection to it, having spent the past three years of my life there as a student midwife. I know the layout, I know the wards, and, best of all, I know the staff. Everyone has been amazingly supportive, kind and encouraging, and I'm sure that is going to continue as I take my first steps in my career.

Career.

Yes, it is terrifying, it really is.

I turn away from the mirror, straighten my tunic, and pick up my bag. It's time to set off. This is it.

I reach the front of the hospital at ten past seven. My shift doesn't start until half-past, but I want time to settle, have a cup of tea, and talk to my mentor before we begin. In all honesty, I know I am going to need to calm my nerves. I'm trying to keep myself together, trying to keep that anxiety at bay. Touch wood I haven't had a bad episode over the last few months, but today is a *Big Day*. That's an understatement: it's an absolutely massive day. I'm taking my time, and taking everything step by step. I can do this.

Somehow the entire hospital seems bigger today, looming ahead of me as I get off the bus and walk towards the entrance. There are more people around than I expected, and I have to wait to let a man using crutches through the main doors. He's followed by a lady pushing an older woman in a wheelchair, and I stand while they pass. The hospital never stops. There are always patients coming and going, even at this time of day. My eyes are drawn over to the clock behind reception. Quarter past. It's fine. No need to rush. No need to worry. Everything is fine.

I take the lift to the Margaret Beresford Unit – the official name of our postnatal ward. Although the hospital feels bigger, the space inside lift feels smaller now. Even alone as I am today, it feels as though I don't have enough room to stand, or enough air to breathe.

I take one breath, and then another, keeping a slow, steady rhythm.

Not today, Violet. Not now.

Breathe in, breathe out.

The lift makes a reassuring *bing* noise, and the doors slide open. There it is, ahead of me: the entrance to the Margaret Beresford Unit.

A rush races through me, sending a pins-and-needles tingle to every part of my body. For the briefest of seconds, I am unsteady on my feet, but I've got this. I'm in control. I stand straight, put my hand down onto the name tag that I've got clipped to my tunic pocket, and smile. I am here. I'm a qualified midwife, and this is the first day of my new beginning.

I drop my bag into the locker room and head straight for the kitchen. There's just about room on the top shelf of the hefty industrial fridge for me to squeeze my lunch box. I learned to bring my own food early on in my training when I realised that some days on the ward finding time for a break is near-impossible. Now I always try to make sandwiches or box up leftovers. To reward myself for getting through a stressful first morning I've put a tiny chocolate bar in the tub with my egg roll. The rational side of me knows that everything is going to be just fine, and that I'll earn that reward. The irrational, anxious side of me wobbles slightly as I fill the kettle and put three large square teabags into the steel pot. I've always made the tea when I'm the first of the morning shift onto the ward, not because I was a student and it was somehow my job, but because I enjoy contributing however I can to the team. Today, standing in the kitchen is giving me time to gather myself and let my heart rate settle before I go through to handover.

I'm lost in my thoughts when the kettle clicks off, steam filling the small room. My hands are shaky, so I force myself to hold them out in front of me and steady them before reaching out for the handle and pouring the boiling water into the teapot. It's fine. No mishaps. I pop the lid onto the pot, and count the mugs that I've set on the tray. Should be plenty. Handover is the busiest time of the day. The night staff are getting ready to go home, and the oncoming shift are gearing up to begin. We cram into the office, run through the patients' names and details, and, if there's time, catch up with each other's lives. Often, there isn't time for that at all.

It's been six months since I was on this ward, but as soon as I walk into the midwives' office it's as though I was never away. There are two other midwives sitting in the room when I arrive, one at the computer, apparently looking for some blood test results, and the other sitting with a set of notes on her lap, completing them in clear, delicate handwriting.

"Tea's up," I say, setting the tray down onto the table.

"Violet!" The midwife, who I recognise as Sam, one of the ward Sisters, turns from the computer as she hears my voice. "How are you doing?" Although I feel calm, I must be giving something away in my expression, because a concerned look crosses her face. "Is this your first shift?"

"Is it that obvious?" I smile. "I thought I'd get the shakes out of the way by making myself carry this tray through without dropping it."

"Better to drop the tray than…well, anything else," she grins. "Good to see you. Well done on finishing your course."

"Thanks," I say. "Tea?"

She nods, and I pour a cup for her, and then look over to the other midwife, a quiet but friendly woman called Moira. "Mo? Cuppa?"

"No thanks," she says. "I'm out of here as soon as we get through handover. There's a thing at Ally's school this morning, so I'm heading straight there."

I sometimes forget how lucky I am to only have myself to think about. It's tough, sometimes, trying to manage a work-life balance – even for a young, single person like me. I can't imagine what it would be like trying to juggle a family too. I couldn't even manage to keep a relationship together, so I doubt I'll have to worry about a husband and kids for a while yet.

"Are you back here tonight?" I ask, taking my tea and sitting next to her.

"This was my last shift. Back next week." She gives a straight-faced thumbs up.

I sip my drink and look around the room. Nothing has changed since I was last here. There are the same posters on the wall, reminding us about hand hygiene and the monthly book club. There's a business card for a nail salon tucked in the corner of the pinboard, although everyone who works here has short-filed fingernails by default. I'm lost in thought as someone says my name.

My mentor, Becky, is standing in the doorway, beaming at me.

"Congratulations!" she says, walking over with her arms extended for a hug.

I set my mug down and awkwardly embrace her.

Becky. I'm so pleased that she is going to be my preceptorship mentor. It's strange to see her here, on the postnatal ward, because she was my supervisor on antenatal during my training. Just as I rotated around the unit for my placements, so most midwives continue to switch wards in practice. There are a few core staff that stay on antenatal, postnatal or delivery, but that's the exception rather than the norm.

"Hey Becky," I say. "Thanks. I just made tea."

"That's one point to you already then," she says. "I'm gasping. You know when you set your alarm for six, with all the good intentions in the world to get up straight away, have a shower, and –" She pauses, looking at me. "No, me neither."

We both laugh. I have learned to become a 'morning person', but I know exactly what she means.

"So, what's new?" Becky asks, when she's poured her tea and taken a seat at the desk.

"Everything feels new, to be honest." I hear a slight waver in my voice. "I moved to a new flat over the weekend, and here I am today."

"You are going to be just fine, Vi," she says.

"I remember my first day," Sam says. "A long, long time ago."

She doesn't look much older than forty, so I'm sure she's exaggerating.

"Another girl from my group started on the same day as me. Katie, or Cathy, I can't remember. She went home at the end of the shift and never came back."

I didn't think things like that actually happened. I can feel my stomach turn over as the words sink in. Some people do give up. It is possible to fail, even now that I'm qualified.

"You'll scare Violet away!" Becky says in semi-jest.

Sam shakes her head. "I tell you what. It made me even more determined to succeed. I didn't want to be like that. I left nursing to train as a midwife and after putting myself through all that I wasn't going to give up. I don't think anything bad actually happened to her to make her leave. She just couldn't cut it."

"Didn't she work that out while she was training?" I ask, trying to smile.

"You'll soon find out that being a student and being a qualified midwife are very different things," Sam says.

Becky cuts in, "And that's why you have a mentor to help you."

I'm thankful for her presence, and for her words. Sam really isn't helping me to keep my anxiety under control. My pulse is fluttering as though I have butterflies not only in my tummy, but in every part of my body.

I look away and drink some of my tea, trying to distract my thoughts from the quavering.

Sam turns back to the computer, oblivious, and Becky pats my knee gently.

"You're going to be absolutely fine," she says.

"Thanks, Becky," I reply.

I want to say more, but I don't know what else to say at the moment. We will have time though. I know I can always talk to Becky.

Because I am supernumerary at present the Sister doesn't allocate me any patients directly. Instead, she gives Becky a slightly greater proportion of the women and babies on the ward, with the assumption that there are two of us to do the work. I need my PIN before I can do any real midwifery duties. I can't sign any paperwork for myself, and I definitely can't be giving out any controlled drugs. There are other limitations, of course, and it feels a little like being in a state of limbo. I'm qualified, I'm here, but I can't do the job I have trained for. Not yet. I'm dressed in my half-way uniform and I have a clumsy sticker over my name badge that reads *'pre-registration midwife'*. It sounds peculiar, and I'm not sure that most of the women on the ward will understand what it means. As Becky and I introduce ourselves to the patients, I end up explaining to each of them that yes, I am a qualified midwife, but I'm new, and limited in what I can do right now.

As it happens, the shift turns out to be a breeze. I have time to do the parts of the job that I enjoy – listening to women, and supporting them in the basic skills that sometimes, even as a student midwife I didn't have time enough to do. After accompanying Becky on the drugs round, I pop in to see Kiera, one of the younger mums on the ward.

She's reading a magazine as I pull back the corner of the curtains and pop my head in.

"Is it a good time, or shall I come back?" I ask.

She smiles. "Teddy is awake, but he's quiet at the moment," she says. "It hasn't happened often so far."

She's pale, and tired looking, but her blood test results have all been fine. No anaemia.

"Did you want to try to take a nap while he's settled?" I ask. "There won't be any visitors on the ward for a few hours yet."

"I'm not sleepy," she says. "Tired, but not sleepy. You know what I mean?"

I step into the curtained-off area, and pull the gap closed behind me.

"Welcome to motherhood," I smile.

"I know you said that you can't do midwife-things yet, because you haven't got your registration or whatever," she says. "Can you do something for me though? If you're allowed. Would you show me how to bath him?"

"Has he fed recently?" I ask. I don't want to bath him too soon after he's had a feed.

"About an hour ago. I snuggled him for a while, and then settled him down in there." She points towards the clear Perspex cot where he is lying, wide-awake, looking peaceful.

"Okay then," I say. "Sure, we can bath him. I'll go down to the nursery room and get everything ready, and then come back for the two of you."

"What do I need to bring?" she asks.

"I'm pretty sure we have everything here," I say. "Although I've been away from the ward for a little while, so I'll go and check."

Keira nods and thanks me.

Midwifery isn't always about delivering babies, writing copious reams of paperwork, giving drugs, or carrying out check-ups. Sometimes it's about the little things that mean a lot more than you ever thought they could. The last few weeks of my training were spent in a blur of getting boxes checked, making sure I had carried out enough examinations of women and babies, and carrying out enough deliveries to get me through the course. Now that's behind me. I really feel like I can get back to learning how to be a midwife. I remind myself the meaning behind the word: midwife – "with woman". That was why I wanted to follow this career path. I wanted to support women, to care for them, be with them, and empower them during this, one of the most important, intimate times of their life.

I toss these thoughts over in my head as I part-fill a baby bath with warm water, and lay two soft white towels on top of the radiator. The nursery room is peaceful, an oasis of calm in an otherwise busy ward. I have rarely had the opportunity to spend time bathing babies with mothers. Much as I would love to do this regularly, it's a task often passed on to healthcare assistants, as midwives get stuck into ward rounds and paperwork. I feel privileged to be able to do this today.

I trail my fingers through the water, feeling its calming warmth against my skin, and then gently dip my elbow in to check the temperature. It's perfect.

When I get back to Keira to fetch her to the nursery she is standing eagerly by the cot, with a dressing gown over her soft grey pyjamas.

"I've got spare clothes for him, and a nappy." She points beneath the cot into the trolley area below.

"Super," I say. "Everything's ready if you two are."

"Yep. Let's go."

Keira had a forceps delivery a couple of days ago, and she walks at a slow, delicate pace, pushing the cot trolley.

"How is it feeling?" I ask, nodding towards her bottom half. "You're okay walking?"

"Sore, but better than yesterday," she says. "I had those painkillers earlier, and they help."

"That's good," I tell her. "The pain and swelling will go down in the next few days."

I hold the nursery door open, and she wheels the trolley into the room.

"This is lovely," she says. "I wish I had a nursery like this at home."

It's nothing special. It's clean and warm, but the walls are painted an institutional shade of white, and the floor is an unimpressive blue vinyl.

"You can undress him now," I say.

It crosses my mind for a moment to ask whether she has her own place, or whether she's by herself, but somehow it doesn't seem like the right way to ask her. She's a teenager, younger than I, and yet here she is, with this gorgeous little human that she's created and given birth to.

I bite back the question and ask instead, "Have you got someone to help you with this at home?"

She carries on getting Teddy undressed while we chat. It feels so natural to be able to talk like this.

"My mum lives around the corner," she says. "I'm with my boyfriend, but he'll be at work during the day, so…" She shrugs. "Mum's great though. Or at least she is now she's got over the shock of being a grandma." Keira smiles in a way that looks calm and comfortable.

I got all the information I wanted without asking in a way that might have raised a barrier between us.

"He's lovely," I say, as she lifts her bare son into her arms.

"Thanks," she replies. "He is pretty cute, isn't he? Would you mind showing me what to do this time?" she asks.

"No, that's fine," I say, and she passes him across.

I hadn't realised how much I'd missed the weight of a baby in my arms until I receive him. There's something indescribably special about holding a new-born.

I talk Keira through the process of bathing Teddy, showing her how to hold him securely, how to use cotton wool to wipe him, and which areas need to be wiped. Not once does Teddy cry or look at all uncomfortable; he's the perfect demonstration model.

When I've finished, Teddy is clean, and Keira is happily chatting away.

"Could you lay one of those towels down in the cot, please?" I nod towards the radiator.

"Sure," she says.

She places a towel into the cot, and I place Teddy on top of it.

"You look like you've been doing that for years," Keira says.

"Well, my training was three years, but that's it," I smile. "You'll get the hang of it in no time. You don't need to bath him more than twice a week, but if you’re still here next time you want to do it, I’ll watch you instead if you like?”

“Thanks, Violet. I’m hoping to get home though really.”

I can’t help but feel a pang of disappointment. It’s silly, of course. I should be happy that she is recovering well, and that she wants to get home to her boyfriend, her mum, and her future with Teddy. I am happy, but the flip side of spending time with mums and babies on the ward is that they leave, and you never know what happens to them. The relationships we build are sometimes long, strong bonds that continue from the antenatal period through to the postnatal days, but more often than not, we see only snapshots of women’s lives.

I know one thing though – my arms are steady, and my mind is focussed. There’s not a trace of that anxiety and nervousness that I had when I was making the tea this morning. I held Teddy confidently; I chatted to Keira and gave her the support she needed. I may not be a fully-fledged PIN-wielding midwife yet, but I *am* a midwife.

At the end of the shift, when we have taken our turn handing over to the afternoon staff, Becky calls me over.

“How are you feeling?” she asks.

It’s the right question.

"Pretty good," I say. "I have to admit, I was super-nervous this morning, but, well, it's been much better than I expected."

"I'm pleased to hear it. I'm going to be honest with you. You're going to have good days and bad days. Remember that I'm here for you, and if you need to talk anything through, anything at all, you let me know. Okay?"

"Thanks, Becky. See you for more tomorrow."

I'm about to turn for the door when she speaks again.

"I mean anything, okay Violet? If you start to get any of that anxiety back, you know that you can talk to me."

I do. Becky has been there for me before, and I have complete faith that I could talk to her again if I need to. I hope that it won't be necessary.

I want to hug her, just like when she walked in this morning. Instead, I nod once, thank her again, and leave.

I have a great job, a super mentor, and I need to get home and phone my awesome best friend and tell her all about it.

## Chapter Three

Even though there are a lot of changes going on in my life, when I snuggle down on my sofa with a huge mug of tea and call Zoe I am instantly reminded that her life is even more tumultuous than mine.

She answers the phone with a breathless *hello*.

"Bad time?" I ask, trying to mask the disappointment in my voice.

"Of course not." She inhales deeply and audibly, and says, more calmly, "How was your first day?"

"What's up?" I want to tell her that it was fine, no, that it was great, and I don't know what I was worrying about, but I know when there's something going on.

"No, you go first," she says. "I'll tell you all about it in a minute. Come on, come on. I've been dying to hear from you."

Even though she can't see me, I smile. This is so like her. We could probably spend the next quarter of an hour arguing about who should speak first, and I know we will if I don't begin. I rush through the details though, knowing that whatever she has to tell me must be more important.

"My mentor is great," I tell her. "That Becky from antenatal, remember I told you about her helping me with my anxiety?"

“She was the one who got you to do your elective day with the mental health specialist midwife?”

“That’s the one.” I’m always impressed with how much Zoe remembers. My mind is like a sieve sometimes. “Anyway, we had a good chat, and I pretty much followed her around doing the basics most of the day. Then I helped a young mum to bath her baby.”

“Awh,” Zoe gushes. “That must be one of the perks of the job, eh?”

“It was nice to have the time to spend,” I say. I want to explain to her just how much it touched me but somehow, I can’t find the way to put my emotions into words.

“I know what you mean,” she says, and I believe it. “I’ve had more time to spend with the kids while I’ve been settling in. I wish we could always work like this.”

In many ways her job as a newly qualified teacher and mine as midwife are very similar.

“Me too,” I say. “I know I’ll be rushed off my feet as soon as I get my PIN. I’m kind of hoping it takes a while to come through.”

“And kind of wishing it were here already?”

“You know it,” I laugh.

“I’m glad it was a good start, Vi. I was worried about you.”

“We both were,” Luke says in the background at Zoe’s end of the phone.

"Thanks, Luke," I say. "No need to worry, but thanks."

Zoe passes on my words, and I take my opportunity to move the conversation back to her.

"So, what's happened?"

"We didn't get the venue we wanted," she says, her voice sinking like a poorly cooked souffle.

"Oh Zo, I'm sorry. I know you had your heart set on The Orangery."

"I should have known that they wouldn't be able to fit us in. They're booked out until next June, and, well, I don't want to wait another year."

"I've tried to tell her there's no rush." Luke again, still hovering.

"I *know*," Zoe tells him. "I really, really, really want a Christmas wedding though. Next year seems so far away."

I hear the sound of a kiss, and again I smile, unseen.

I'm settling into a new home and new job, but at least I'm not trying to plan a wedding at three months' notice. We've spent hours, maybe days, poring over ideas boards on Pinterest, browsing through bridal magazines and wedding planner websites. Luke has nodded and made enthusiastic noises at everything that Zoe has shown him, but at the end of the day, whatever she chooses is what will happen. I get to be bridesmaid, so I am experiencing the vicarious thrills of planning without personally having to go through a ceremony. It's much like being a midwife, where I get to share in the experience of childbirth and newborn babies without carrying and caring for my own. If only there were a way that I could experience a large glass of wine without any of the negative effects, I might just have the perfect life.

"What about the other options?" I've curled up in a foetal position on the sofa now, tucking my legs up to fit into the space.

"There's Harcroft Hall, and Cranbourne Acres."

"Cranbourne Acres," I repeat. "That was the one with the glass-walled walkway?" I do remember *some* things, it seems.

"Uh-huh," she says. Her voice lacks enthusiasm, but I'm sure it's the disappointment of not getting her first choice, rather than any reflection on the suitability of the other venue.

"We can go and have a look," I say. "If you want to. Unless you and Luke…"

"I'll see what he thinks," Zoe replies.

It was me and Zoe for so long that I forget sometimes that this wedding is about her and Luke. I'm the bridesmaid, the helper, the friend, and I'm going to have to keep myself in check. Luke and I are good friends; I don't want to make him feel pushed out of his own arrangements.

"Sure," I say. "But Zo, don't worry. You will find somewhere perfect, I know it. Things happen for a reason. I know how much you wanted The Orangery, but wait and see, something wonderful is going to come up."

"It's usually me telling you not to worry," Zoe laughs. "But okay. I'll try to believe you."

"You're usually right too," I say.

Luke and Zoe have been a couple for two years, which seems like a long time at our age. He was the third housemate in our student accommodation, and, although it took them a year to manage to get it together, they hit it off right from our first day of living at Tangiers Court. Thinking back to those days makes me well up with a sad nostalgia. It was barely three years ago that I was starting my midwifery training, and now here I am, at the beginning of my career. There were times that I thought I wasn't going to make it. My anxiety and self-doubt threatened to derail my hopes of success so often, but I had Zoe, I had Becky, and I had other friends along the way who helped me, supported me, and gave me the strength to believe in myself. And then there was That Guy.

As soon as the thought enters my mind, my sad nostalgia melts into sad anger.

Twenty-one years old. Single. Alone. Alone. Alone.

I scrunch up my eyes, pressing them tightly to hold back the stupid tears that want to come out. I won't let them.

When I open my eyes again, I take a good long look around the room. My living room. My flat. Yes, okay, it's a rented flat. It's not like I own it or anything, but this is my home. I pay the rent, I'll be paying the bills, I'll be making the decisions. If I want to come in from work and sit in my penguin pyjamas watching *Cooking Queens*, I can do that. If I want to stick a spoon into a full tub of *Ben and Jerry's* and devour the whole pot, I can do that. I mean, I'd better not do that too often, but if I want to, I can. If I want to lie in the bath for three hours, reading a book, listening to Adele songs, I can do that.

There won't be anyone here to hug me and listen to me when I get home after a bad day, but perhaps I don't need that. I have Zoe at the other end of the phone line. She lives ten minutes away, and if I ever do need her, she'll be here. I try to look for the positives, but my thoughts slip so easily to the negatives. That's how my brain works; it always lets me down. Zoe will always be there for me, but maybe I should stop being so dependent on her. My thoughts head in that direction and I can't stop them. She's getting married soon. She has her life, and I have mine. I can't just call her up whenever I have a hard day on the ward. I'm not her responsibility.

I was feeling much better when I was thinking about all the ice-cream that I was definitely not going to eat. It's only my third day living in the flat, being away from Zoe, being on my own. Feeling like this must be normal. Mustn't it?

# Chapter Four

On Wednesday, I'm back into work for a late shift – my second day on the ward. As soon as I walk through the double doors onto the unit, I know that I'm not going to be having the same kind of easy day that I had yesterday.

"If you see the paediatrician, grab him," one of the midwives says, hurrying up the ward away from the office.

"Sure," I call after her.

"Don't let him go," she says, over her shoulder, as she keeps walking.

"Okay." I raise my voice to be heard, but try not to turn it into a shout.

"She'll be lucky," Diane, one of the afternoon shift midwives laughs. "Have you seen the discharge list? Paeds have been up in NICU with the triplets all morning."

Paeds. NICU. So many things get turned into abbreviations and acronyms here. When I first started I would have taken a few minutes to work out that she meant the paediatricians have been on the Neonatal Intensive Care Unit.

"Triplets?" I ask. If I had been on the unit over the past few months, or even weeks, I'd have known there were triplets due. The mother would have been booked to have an elective Caesarean, and we would have known to expect her. I guess that everyone else did know.

"Thirty-two weeks. She did well to get to that too. They're stable, don't look so worried."

So often I forget to keep a check on the way I show my emotions.

"They'll be staying there a while?" I ask the question even though I know the answer.

"As long as they need to. Anyway, Mum isn't up from recovery yet, but we can't clear any beds because paeds aren't free to discharge any of the babies."

Some of the midwives are qualified to carry out baby checks. There is an abundance of post-registration courses available for us to learn additional skills, and specialise in various areas. I'm guessing that today is one of those days that we aren't fortunate enough to have a midwife on duty that has taken her examination of the newborn course. What will I do? For now, I will focus on getting through this shift. My future career plans can wait until I've got the present under control.

"Violet," Becky rests her hand on my shoulder from behind. "Best have a cup of tea now. I don't think we'll get a break for a while."

I smile, fully aware that I must look as nervous as I feel.

"Okay," I say.

"It'll be fine. We'll be busy, but it will be fine."

I nod, and walk to the kitchen. As I lean against the worktop, I can hear the hubbub of the ward behind me, through the closed door. Women talking, at least two babies crying, doors opening, closing, fast-paced footsteps in the corridor. A fierce dizziness grips me, and I lower my head to my chest, willing it to pass. Yesterday's peaceful, pleasant shift lulled me into a sense of serene security. Today, I'm going to be stretched, and probably stressed.

"There's no time for this." I speak the words out loud, stressing each syllable firmly and as calmly as I can manage. "Violet Cobham, you have a job to do."

I take a gulping breath and shake my hands out in front of me, trying to release the tension that I can feel darting through my body.

There aren't that many places on the ward where it's possible to be alone and have a few moments of reflection. The kitchen is usually one of them. Today though someone clatters through the door, just as I finish speaking to myself. I'm thankful they didn't come in a few seconds earlier. I feel bad enough being the new girl without people thinking that I'm not quite right.

"Violet!"

It's Geri Smith, one of the senior midwives: my former postnatal placement mentor.

"Geri!" I'm as happy to see her as she appears to be to see me. "How are you? Hello!"

I instinctively reach out to hug her, but she grins and pats my arm instead.

"I don't hug much," she says. "But it's great to have you back."

Undeterred, I smile broadly.

"Are you on the late shift?" I ask.

"Unfortunately," she says. "Looks like hell out there."

With a slow nod, I give a tight-lipped agreement.

She looks down at my badge, where the clumsy sticker denotes me as 'pre-registration', and says, "I think there will be plenty for you to do today. Pre-registration or not."

I want to do my share. I've passed my course, and I'm qualified. Without my PIN though, my hands are tied.

"Whatever I'm allowed to do, I will," I tell her.

"I know, Violet. You're a hard worker. I trained you well."

Geri certainly played a role in the way that I developed during my training. Although some of the students cast her in the role of one of the 'scary' midwives, and none of the others wanted to work with her, I learned some valuable lessons from Geri's tough-love approach. I'm glad she's here. I really am.

Although the ward is full, Janet, the morning shift Sister, runs through handover as quickly as possible. I can already tell by the details that she provides that several of the women and their babies are fit, well, and ready to go home. All they need is that check from the paediatrician to clear the infants for discharge.

"But you know the situation with the paeds," Janet says with a sigh. "As soon as they come you'll be able to empty some beds. Delivery suite have three ladies waiting to transfer, but I think one of them might go for early discharge home if there's much more of a delay."

"Are all the sections up from this morning? Apart from the triplet mum?"

A part of me still cringes at the way that even the most sensitive and caring of midwives can fall into the habit of referring to women as 'sections' or 'the triplet mum', rather than by name or as individual people. There's something dehumanising about reducing these women to their conditions or medical statuses. I find it difficult enough to call them 'patients' rather than 'mums', but then again I was never a nurse. I've never worked on a general ward, and I never plan to. Midwives like Janet and Geri trained as nurses, and worked on surgical wards, medical wards, in surgery or in clinics before taking the additional midwifery training. As I can't carry out midwifery duties yet, all I can do is support women, care for them and their babies, and do the tasks around the ward that often go unnoticed but contribute to the way that it runs.

"Delivery suite is full, but there aren't any more planned sections," Janet says. "Who knows though?"

There's a collective groan. It's impossible to know.

Becky is up on her feet, beckoning me to follow her as soon as handover is finished.

"Busy, busy," she says. "Don't worry though. I know it seems like we have a lot to do, but this is good practice in time management and planning."

"I wish I could help out more," I tell her.

"I'm sure there will be plenty for you to do. We'll go and see the ladies and then work out what needs doing with the discharge paperwork. I don't want to wait hours for the paeds and then find out we're waiting on blood results or whatever."

She walks down the corridor towards the end of the ward that we will be working on today. We have ten women and their babies to care for. Even though I'm supernumerary, Geri allocated us more women than herself and the other midwife on shift. In a couple of hours, the ward should be less full, and we should be less busy. Should be. Who knows?

There are medications to give out, blood pressure and other physical checks to undertake, and, most importantly, we talk to each of the women as we make our way around the ward. It feels like half an hour, but by the time we make it back to the office to check the paperwork an hour and a half has passed. There's still no sign of a paediatrician.

I'm about to sit down with Becky to look through the discharge packs when Geri walks into the office.

"Could you help Vic with some beds down my end please, Violet?" she says.

I look at Becky for confirmation, just as I used to when I was a student, before remembering that I don't need to check in with my placement supervisor anymore. I'm a qualified midwife now.

"Sure," I say. There aren't many tasks that I'm allowed to do yet, but this is one of them. "You'll be okay with the paperwork?" I ask Becky.

"No worries," she says. Then she turns to Geri and asks, "Have some of the women been discharged?"

Geri shakes her head. "No. Bed four has got up for a bath and she's staying another couple of days. She needs her bed changing. The woman next to her had her toddler visiting and he's spilled juice all over her sheets, so…" She doesn't finish the sentence, but gives an exasperated wave of her hands instead. "As if we don't have enough to do. Sort her out too, please."

"It's fine," I say, getting to my feet. Bed four, you say?"

"Thanks love," Geri says.

Vic, the maternity assistant, has already stripped bed four by the time I arrive, and she's wiping over the waterproof blue mattress cover.

"Alright?" I say with a smile.

"There'll be lots of this today," she says, without stopping.

I take the left edges of the flat sheet, Vic takes the right, and we set about making the bed.

The ward around us is buzzing with chatter and clatter. It's visiting time, and even though we try to keep numbers to a minimum so that those mums that need rest can get it, nearly every bedspace is packed. This end of the ward is Nightingale-style: a row of beds on each side of the ward, separated only by thick blue institutional curtains. There's just about enough privacy for women to have a little time to themselves, but there's no soundproofing. Hovering below the hubbub, I can hear quiet crying. It's coming from the bed next to us.

I look up at Vic, to see if she's heard what I can hear. She doesn't make any signs that she's aware of the low sobbing. There's another sheet and a blanket to lay down, and the pillowcases need replacing.

Leaning over the bed, I whisper. "Do you hear crying?"

She tilts her head, like a dog trying to tune in to a distant noise.

"Babies? Lots of them, yes."

There's one baby crying, for sure, but that's not what I meant.

"A mother," I say.

She cocks her head the other way. It's possible that she can't hear the woman, as I think the sound is coming through the curtain nearest to me. Vic shakes her head.

I look at the sheets, then at Vic, and quickly make a mental plan. If I get this done I can talk to the woman within a couple of minutes, and Vic won't be left doing this on her own. Or I can pop my head around the curtain immediately, and tell the woman that I'll be with her as soon as I can. Or perhaps I should tell Vic I need to talk to the woman now and leave her to finish the top covers by herself.

It shouldn't feel like such a dilemma, but I am new, I'm inexperienced, and I still need to learn a lot about decision making and prioritising.

While I've been thinking, Vic and I have laid the top sheet. There's only the blanket and pillowcases left to go. I take the edge of the blanket, tuck it neatly, as I've been taught, and smooth it down.

"Would you mind finishing the pillows, and I'll see what's up next door?" I ask.

Vic shrugs.

"Sure," she says, already picking up one of the waterproof covered pillows as I duck out.

I stand outside the curtain around the neighbouring bedspace, and take a short deep breath before pulling back the corner slightly. I dip my head inside at first.

"Hey," I say. "I'm Violet. I'm…" I almost say that I'm a student midwife because I'm so used to speaking the words. But what am I? A midwife? She might want things that I can't do because I've not got my PIN yet. A pre-registration midwife? She's obviously upset and having to explain everything isn't going to help. "I'm working on the ward," I say.

The woman is sitting in the uncomfortable wooden-framed chair at the side of the bed, dabbing at her eyes with a tissue.

"I'm sorry," she says. "Was I making a lot of noise? I was trying to be quiet. I didn't want to disturb anyone."

I shake my head, and enter the bedspace, pulling the curtain closed behind me.

"Not at all," I tell her. "What's wrong? Would you like to talk about it?"

Her baby is lying fast asleep in the cot at the other side of the bed. I'm trying to remember from handover what the woman's name is, how many days postnatal she is, and whether she had any problems that I should know about. I listen during handover, and I take notes, but when the ward is full, once I've been allocated a set of women I don't always remember everything about everyone else on the ward. I make a mental note to try harder in future.

"I just feel so – stupid," she says. "Jacob came in to see me. My husband brought our son to meet his little brother, and Jacob got a bit over-excited."

"And he spilled his juice," I say, filling in the details.

"I can see how busy it is, and I feel like I'm wasting everyone's time. I shouted at Jacob, and now I feel terrible about that too. His first time seeing Felix, and he's only going to remember how Mummy shouted at him." Her tears had settled, but as she speaks the floods begin again, and she lets out a large, honking cry.

I take a seat on the edge of the stripped blue mattress.

"I can tell you that you are not wasting our time," I say. I reach into the tissue box on her bedside table, and hand her a fresh replacement for the rag that she is wiping her eyes with. "These things happen. It's part of our job to make sure you're comfortable."

"You're so busy though. I can see how full it is."

I shake my head again. "That doesn't matter. It looks busy, but a lot of the women here are just waiting to go home."

"I want to go home too," she says. "I want to be at home with Jacob and Felix and my husband. I don't want to be here anymore."

She's crying harder now, and I'm not sure how much I am helping. I wrack my brain trying to remember why this lady has to stay. It's no use. I reach into my pocket and pull out my handover sheet as she tries to dry her eyes.

Leanne King. Third day post Caesarean. Waiting for blood results. Low haemoglobin. Might need a transfusion. Second baby, well, okay I know that.

"I'll talk to Geri, the midwife who's looking after you," I tell her. "Looks like we're waiting on your blood results?"

Leanne nods.

"I know it must be very difficult being away from your family, and you must miss Jacob a lot."

She wipes her nose and snorts back more tears.

"But I'm sure that all he is going to remember is seeing his new baby brother, and how excited he is to have both of you home with him. We'll do everything we can to get you home to him as soon as possible. We just need to make sure that you're well enough to leave us. Okay?"

"I want to go home," she says again.

"Oh, Leanne. I understand." I think for a few seconds. "Were you feeling alright before your family came in?"

"I'm a bit wobbly on my feet, but, yes, pretty much."

"Were you, er, upset, before? Or feeling down?"

She shrugs. "A little maybe. Like I said, I really want to get home now. There was a woman down the corridor who had her section on the same day as me and she's gone home this morning."

She was lucky to get the baby discharged before the paeds got busy, I think but don't say.

"It can be normal to get what people sometimes call 'the Baby Blues' on the third or fourth day after delivery," I tell her. "You don't need me to tell you how draining it is, having your baby. Your emotions can take a bit of a battering with all the hormones too."

It's her turn to pause for a moment.

"I remember that from when I had Jacob, yes."

"Did it pass in a few days?"

She nods. "Oh yes. I didn't have postnatal depression or anything. I was just…I don't even know if I was really sad, I suppose I was tearful. Emotional, yes. Do you think that's what this is?"

"It is common to feel that way," I say. "And normal. If it gets worse, if you do start to feel at all depressed, there's a lot of support available. But at the moment, try not to be too hard on yourself for shouting at your little boy."

"He did seem fine afterwards," she says, appearing to settle slightly. "And he gave me a huge hug before he left. Oh, he smells so sweet. I miss the feel of him in my arms. I call him my little teddy bear because he's so cuddly." She breaks out into a smile.

"Maybe I'll get to meet him before you leave," I say, smiling back. "Look, I'll let your midwife Geri know that we had a chat, and I'll try to chase up those blood results for you, okay?"

"Okay," Leanne replies.

"If you want to talk some more, grab me, or any of the other staff. And please don't think you're wasting anyone's time. No matter how busy, we're here for you."

"Okay," she says again. "And thanks, Violet."

I place my hand gently on hers and give it a pat that I hope is reassuring rather than patronising.

"Shall I get Vic to come and help me make your bed?" I ask. "Or would you like us to give you a few minutes?"

Leanne straightens herself up, and wipes her red eyes a final time.

"Nope. I'm going to be alright. You go ahead."

Her smile is brave and unforced, and I can't help but smile back again. I'm sure she's right. I believe she's going to be just fine.

By the time Vic and I have finished making up Leanne's bed, her spirits appear to have improved. I make a mental note to remember to check her blood results, or at least to prompt Geri to do it. The curtained area around her bed has offered a temporary respite against the chaos of the ward, but as we leave the cocoon and broach the main area again we are hit by the cacophony of mums, dads, babies, visitors and…

"Violet. There you are. Can you run down to the lab with these samples, please?" Geri stands in front of me, waving three clear plastic bags, each containing an array of blood-filled tubes.

The usual protocol is to call for a porter. These bloods are either urgent or late.

"Uh, sure," I say. This is another of those non-midwifery jobs that I can do while I'm in the pale blue instead of the navy. I can see through the clear plastic of the bag that one of the samples belongs to Leanne.

"The lady, er, Leanne, was asking about her blood results," I tell Geri. "She was feeling a bit weepy, but she seems better now. I had a chat with her."

"Good, good," says Geri, looking over my shoulder towards the bed she was clearly heading for. "Hurry then. Let's get those bloods down so she can get her results."

Geri means well, I know she does. She might come across as sharp and abrupt, but she's one of the most efficient midwives that I had the pleasure to work with whilst I was a student. In many ways, she's the direct opposite to my preceptorship mentor, Becky. Geri is a no-nonsense, hard truth kind of woman, while Becky is emotionally driven and intuitive. Both of them supported me when I was on placement with them, and both of them taught me things about midwifery and about myself.

I don't say anything else; there seems little point. Instead, I take the blood samples and leave the ward. Part of me feels bad that I'm not there, lending a hand, listening to the women who might not otherwise be heard today. Part of me is relieved that I have a ten-minute break from the rush and bustle. I'm fairly sure it's the only break I'll be having today.

# Chapter Five

I hurry back to the ward as quickly as possible after delivering the samples to the lab. I've probably been no more than quarter of an hour, but I'm greeted on my return by Becky.

"Where have you been? Can you sort the paperwork out for bed twelve? Paeds said they're on the way up, and she hasn't got her pack." She sounds out of breath, and her face has the rosy glow that comes with being on one's feet for nearly four hours. We're only halfway through the shift, and it feels like it's never going to end.

I don't bother answering the first question. Instead, I nod.

"Sure, no problem."

Putting the postnatal paperwork together will give me a few minutes to sit down. I'll take it.

Becky pats my arm, and walks purposefully back down the corridor towards our assignment of women.

The discharge pack includes some notes for the postnatal care the woman will receive from the community team, a child health record, and a bundle of useful information leaflets. On quiet days, putting together the packs is one of the tasks that we all chip in with. There's usually a stack of pre-prepared envelopes in the stationery cupboard. When there's a busy period the packs fly out of the cupboard quicker than we can replace them, and bundling the documents together is yet another task on the non-stop to-do list.

I gather everything quickly, and I'm just pushing it into one of the large brown envelopes when a youthful-looking doctor with drooping shoulders arrives at the office doorway.

"Afternoon," he says. "Not sure we've met. I'm Doctor Riley. Robert Riley. Paeds."

As soon as he speaks the magic word I immediately sit to attention.

"Oh gosh. Good," I say. "There are a lot of –"

"I only have ten minutes," he cuts in. "I finish at half six, so..." He leaves the rest of the sentence hanging, but I can fill in the rest.

"Right." Prioritise, Violet. Who's the most in need of review? Think.

"I'll handover the discharges," Riley says. "You had a baby that was jaundiced? He was on the BiliBed?"

The BiliBed looks very much like a mini sunbed. Jaundiced babies are laid beneath the UV light to help them to break down the bilirubin in their blood that can form in the early days after birth and make them turn the orangey-yellow shades of jaundice. He's down Geri's end of the ward, so I haven't seen him this afternoon, and I have to pull my handover notes out of my pocket again to confirm the bed number.

"Side room," I say. "Second on the left."

Riley nods, and turns almost as soon as I have finished speaking.

"We really need those discharges," I call after him. "Some of the women have…"

There's no point carrying on. He's gone. Our conversation was a truncated mess, but at least is he here. For ten minutes.

I pause to take a breath and enjoy the sensation of sitting down for a few more seconds. Then I gather up the discharge pack and place it with the lady in bed twelve's hospital file. She's ready to go as soon as the paediatrician – or one of the paediatricians – says so.

Again, I'm in two minds. Should I go and find Geri and tell her that the doctor is on the ward reviewing the jaundiced baby, or should I return to Becky and help her out? Becky must have been on her own down our end of the ward while I've been changing beds and playing at being a porter. I feel that digging in with her is the right thing to do.

I stretch my arms out, shake the tension from my tired legs and walk down the ward to find her.

Becky is with a tall, dark-haired woman, rolling up the sleeve on a red-dotted pyjama top to measure her blood pressure.

"Hi Violet," Becky says. "Yvonne was feeling a little light-headed."

Yvonne's face is ghostly pale, but she looks up at me and gives a small smile.

"Sorry," she says. "Didn't mean to waste your time, ladies."

Becky shakes her head, just as I had earlier when Leanne said much the same thing to me. Wasting our time. Is that what these women really think? The thought hits me hard, like a thudding blow to my heart.

"Not at all," Becky reassures her. "I need to check you're okay. This is what we are here for."

I give my best, most genuine smile, and hope the warmth that I feel comes across. The last thing I ever want is for the women I support and care for – care about – to think that they're wasting my time. Even if I barely have a minute to sit, if I'm rushed off my feet, I never want to make anyone feel that way.

"Er, Becky," I say, as soon as the blood pressure machine has stopped whirring. The reading is fine. "The paediatrician turned up while I was finishing that paperwork."

"At last," Becky sighs. "That's great, thanks."

"Not so great," I reply. "He was in a rush. He's handing over to the next shift. Well, he's actually handing the discharges over to the next shift."

"What?" Becky sounds outraged. I wish I had waited until she had finished monitoring Yvonne. Becky points at the blood pressure monitor. "Seems fine, Yvonne. Stay on your bed for a few minutes and try to rest. We'll get some bloods down to the lab to check your iron levels if that's okay?"

"Yes," she says. "A little more blood can't hurt, eh?" She's smiling broadly now, and it's contagious, despite the tension in the air.

"I'll pop back in a few minutes," Becky tells her.

Without saying anything else to me, she hurries away from Yvonne's bed area in the direction of the other end of the ward.

Should I have been more assertive with Doctor Riley? Was there something else I should have said to him? Should I have gone straight down to tell Geri that he'd arrived, and what he had said? I don't know. I may have learned how to provide midwifery care, but I am already starting to understand that there are a lot more important skills that I have yet to gain. I don't have the experience to make the decisions that I should be able to make.

"You alright, love?" Yvonne says from the bed.

I'd almost forgotten that I was still standing here.

"Er, yes," I say, but it is far from the truth.

Yesterday was a breeze. I chatted to women, I bathed a baby, I thought that being a qualified midwife was the most wonderful thing in the world. Now I can't even make a decision without second-guessing myself.

"Sorry." I smile at Yvonne again, and she nods in return.

"Make sure you get some rest too," she says, and I feel that dull thud against my heart again. I have to get out of her bedspace before I let my emotions break.

Fortunately for me, and most importantly for the women on the ward, Robert Riley is true to his word. Twenty minutes after Riley leaves, the paediatrician that takes over from him arrives. Brenda Carr, a tall, angular woman, wearing a sharp tweed-style dress beneath her white coat, is fresh and raring to go.

"What have you got for me?" she asks in a light, friendly voice.

Geri nods over to the discharge list. There are ten names on the sheet now. Ten mothers and babies waiting to go home. It's just gone seven; we'll be going home ourselves in two and a half hours.

"Okay," Carr says, undeterred. "Let's get going."

As she makes her way around the Perspex cots to carry out the discharge examinations, Becky and I head in the other direction to start another round of maternal check-ups. I've not eaten since I arrived. The aroma of hospital food taunted me when the domestic assistant handed out the women's meals, but my beef sandwich has remained firmly in the fridge. I got a few mouthfuls of tea, but that's as close as I've come to a break.

None of us have managed to sit for long, so I can't complain. We are all in this together. If we push through, and if the paediatrician doesn't find any problems, we can get some, if not most of the waiting women home tonight. If not, well, I'm back here in the morning, and we can do this all over again.

"Are you with me, Vi?" Becky asks.

I'm lagging behind her on the corridor, lost in my thoughts and exhausted by the day. Like a jogger who has only just taken up running, I'm new to the game, and slow. I don't have the stamina that Becky, Geri, and the other midwives do. As a student I was buffered from the constant, unceasing demands of the ward by my status. It seems that this is another thing that I have to learn.

"Right here," I say, quickening my step to catch up.

"It's not always like this." Becky puts her hand on my shoulder and gives me a firm pat.

"But sometimes it is," I reply. I want to smile, but I can't bring myself to find the energy.

My mentor looks at me, says nothing, and nods.

I'm sure I can see something in her expression. A kind of sadness, perhaps, or maybe she is as exhausted as I am, but better at hiding it.

We walk on together in a wordless solidarity, and when we speak to the women under our care we smile.

And we mean it.

Somehow I scramble through to the end of the shift. By the time I get home it's ten thirty, and I'm completely bushed. I stand in the kitchen, a mindless zombie staring into the cupboard trying to decide what to eat. I heat a can of soup, the first food I've had since lunchtime, and throw another can into my bag with the optimistic hope that tomorrow I'll have time to eat at work. Tomorrow. I have nine hours until I need to be back at work. The thought spurs me on to spoon the rest of the steaming cream of chicken into my mouth, throw the dirty bowl into the dishwasher and head straight to bed.

I haven't messaged Zoe, I haven't showered, and I certainly don't have time to worry about whether the morning shift is going to be just as busy as today. My head hits the pillow and I'm gone.

# Chapter Six

My alarm blasts out its beeping blare at half-past six. I stumble to the shower, and as I try to wake myself up, my mind runs through the events of yesterday. It was tough. All of it was tough. I'm not even carrying out midwifery duties; right now, I'm doing even less than I did as a student, and it still feels like too much.

I rub the shampoo into my flat brown hair, rinse, and condition. The soap on my body refreshes my skin, but I still feel exhausted. Resting my head against the smooth cream-coloured tiles I take a deep breath, letting the warm water run over me. I prefer baths to showering, water always soothes me, but this morning, a quick shower is all I have time for, and I only just about have time for that.

Time, time, time.

Is this the way it's going to be from now on? Dashing from shift to home to shift, with nothing else in between? My mind fills with images of everything that happened yesterday. The women desperately waiting to go home, not receiving the attention they deserved, feeling like they were wasting our time if they so much as called one of us. My heart sinks deeper.

Flattening the palms of my hands against the tiled wall, letting its weight support my body. I want to stay in this shower, in my safe little bubble. I don't know if I'm strong enough to spend another full shift on my feet today. I'm not sure I can handle this feeling of letting everyone down. My sinking heart quickens, and I can feel a dizzy lightness start spinning in my brain. I've got to get out of here before my legs turn to jelly and my anxiety has me in a heap.

I knew this would happen, of course I did. The first day made me believe that being a qualified midwife could be sweetness and light, but I should have reminded myself that those days - the peaceful shifts where you can spend all the time you want with the women that need you - they're few and far between. I have twenty minutes to be dried, dressed, and out of the door. I don't have time for this now.

Grabbing hold of the side of the shower door with one hand I reach for my towel with the other and pull it around myself. My body feels like a Jenga tower, precarious and ready to fall at any second. I have to keep the blocks in place, keep myself steady – physically and mentally. Wrapped in the towel I steady myself towards my bedroom and perch on the edge of my bed.

"Come on, Midwife Cobham," I tell myself in a firm, direct voice. "There's work to be done."

I imagine that it's Becky's soft reassurance, encouraging me to push through my feelings.

I picture Geri, her to-the-point bluntness ushering me upwards and onwards.

Then I hear Zoe's voice.

"You can do this," it says. I know that's what she would tell me if she were here.

If we still lived together I could walk across the landing of our shared house into her room, no matter what time of the day, and tell her how I was feeling, how I *am* feeling. Now everything has changed. I'm on my own.

I pull my phone off the bedside table, and type a quick couple of sentences.

**Sorry I didn't message yesterday. Crazy shift.**

I pause. I don't want to worry her, but I do want to talk to her about how I'm feeling. I add to the text.

**Hope you're okay. Chat tonight? xx**

It's not even seven in the morning yet. In her two-bedroomed house down the road, over the roundabout, two streets on the left, Zoe will be waking up. Luke will probably have brought her some coffee, and the two of them will be getting ready to start their day. I'm alone, and today I really wish that I were not.

I stare at the words on the screen for a few seconds, and somehow even messaging Zoe makes me feel a little more stable. I'll talk to her tonight. Whatever happens today, I can get through it. Then tonight I can chat with my best friend.

I didn't expect a reply so soon, but my phone buzzes in my hand, and a message alert pops up.

**Come over after five? I'll make dinner. Today will be a better day. xx**

I gulp back a ball of emotion, and manage to smile slightly as I reply.

**Can't wait to see you xx**

The digital clock on the front of my phone reminds me that I have ten minutes to get to the bus stop. I'm not operating at one hundred percent, but I'm hovering at over seventy now, and that is going to have to get me there. The foggy haze of anxiety is still floating in my brain, but the last thing I can do is miss a shift on my third day. There's work to be done, and I have to push myself.

As I walk onto the unit, I look up and down the ward, trying to garner some indication as to how busy it might be. There are no visible clues. I can see the Nightingale ward areas at either end of the unit, with their curtained-off bays, but there's no way of knowing whether the beds within those bays are occupied. There's one woman holding onto a drip stand, trundling it along the corridor out of the bathroom, towards the bedded area. Her gait is unsteady, but she's making her way without too much difficulty. I don't recognise her from yesterday, so she must have been transferred up overnight.

"Are you coming in, or will you be standing in the corridor today?" One of the support workers nudges me gently with the edge of the tea tray. "Move along," she says, with a smile.

"Sorry," I say. I give a quick glance into the office and then duck into the locker room to leave my bag before joining the room full of staff for handover.

It's not quite the state of bedlam that faced me yesterday. Still, there are enough women and babies on the ward to keep all of us busy. Despite the fact that I am supernumerary, there's only Becky, Moira, two support workers and myself on the shift.

"Good job you're here," Becky grimaces.

"Sal was meant to be on, but she called in sick," Mo explains.

"She must be ill then. Sal would come in if her arm was falling off," Becky laughs.

I've noticed that this is a trend amongst the staff; everyone seems reluctant to take sick days, even if they really seem to need them. It's almost as though they'd rather press on through their pains and personal suffering then let the rest of the team down. Part of me is impressed by their level of commitment to the ward, and to each other, but part of me is worried about the sustainability of this attitude. You can't keep pushing yourself when your body, or mind, need to take a break, surely? There must come a point where you need to put your own health first.

It's going to be another busy shift. Not quite at the level of yesterday's chaos, but it does look as though there won't be much chance to sit down, drink tea and take a breather. Do the ward rounds, give out the drugs, check the babies have fed, and most importantly talk to the women. Spend time with them. Be a midwife: with woman.

Becky and I have eight women and their babies to care for between us. Normal deliveries, waiting to go home. I stop myself, shake my head, dislodge that way of thinking. Women who have had normal deliveries. I can't slip into that medicalised approach; I won't let it happen.

The shift passes in a blur. One minute I'm sitting with a new mum, discussing breastfeeding positions, the next Becky is asking me if I'm almost ready to handover our ladies. I managed to sit down to eat my lunch, even though it was only a quick fifteen minutes rather than the half hour that we are actually allocated. This is where it starts, that putting the ward before yourself ethos. Snatch a quick break, miss your break if you need to. Come in when you're running at eighty per cent. Come in when you're running at twenty per cent. We are a team, and we don't let each other down, but I can't help wondering if I will end up letting myself down.

I'm still helping out right up until my official end time of half past three. I discovered as a student that if I leave dead on time I can make it to the bus stop for the first bus at twenty-five to – otherwise I have to wait a half hour for the next one to arrive. Today fate is smiling in my favour.

I'm home by four. I change out of my uniform, make tea, flop onto the sofa, and turn on the television. Five minutes. I'll just take five minutes, then I'll be recharged enough for my evening with Zoe. Just five minutes.

Somehow I manage to slip into a much-needed nap, and I sleep through the entire episode of *Cooking Queens*. The clock on my phone reads 17:11 as my phone rings to wake me up.

"Where are you?" Zoe's voice sounds out from the other end of the line.

"Ugh, sorry," I say. My words are sleep-slurred and muffled.

"Another busy day?" she asks. "Do you still want to come over?"

"Of course," I reply. I look myself over. "Let me freshen up and I'll be there as soon as I can."

"I would say that there's no hurry, but Luke will be home soon, and I can't guarantee the safety of your share of the curry I've made."

"Well in that case," I say, with a laugh. "I'm on my way."

My dressing table mirror tells me that I look at least a little better than I feel. After I've pulled out my ponytail and brushed my sleep-messed hair I dab a little foundation onto my skin. I could almost pass as human. Late nights, early mornings, no sleep, skirting around the edge of anxiety attacks and looking like, well, not looking so hot: I guess that's my life now. Then again, that's pretty much been my life for the past three years.

"This is what you wanted." I tell mirror-me.

She frowns. I turn my back on her, leave the flat and set off on the walk to Zoe's.

It's the beginning of September, and the evenings are still light. The proximity of my flat to Zoe and Luke's new place wasn't a deciding factor, but it helped me to tip my decision in its favour. There was a cute apartment on the other side of town that boasted sea views, but it was way too far away to be convenient for work or for my bestie. Besides, the sea view was the slightest speck, and you could only see it if the tree across the street was blowing the right way in the wind.

I make it to Zoe's before Luke gets there, and I'm hit by the delicious aroma from the kitchen as soon as my best friend opens the door.

"Hey!" she welcomes me.

"Alright," I say, reaching out for a hug before stepping inside.

Zoe and Luke managed to find an amazing starter home. There's a wide hallway that leads on to the kitchen-diner through one door and to a chic, high-ceilinged living room through another. She walks me straight to the back of the house where I sit at the dining table while she carries on cooking.

I say what I'm thinking.

"You've really struck lucky."

She turns to look at me.

"The house? I know," she says. "I love it so much."

"Not just the house," I reply. "I mean everything. You're so…I don't know. It just feels like you've got everything together, that everything's working out for you. I'm so pleased, Zo."

"Says Miss Midwife over there. Independent. Great job. Lovely flat. Absolutely gorgeous and mind-bogglingly wonderful."

As soon as she turns the compliments back in my direction, I wish I hadn't said anything. I feel the blush hit my skin, and my tongue sits silent in my mouth. She senses the change, sets her wooden spoon onto the chopping board, and takes a step towards me.

"Hey," she says. "It's alright. What's wrong?"

A cool tear runs down my hot cheek, followed by another. Within seconds streams of saltwater slick down my red skin.

"It's…so…hard," I say through choking sobs. "It's non-stop. I thought I was ready, but…" I stop. I don't know what to say. How do I explain that everything that I dreamed of is turning out to be a nightmare?

"I thought you were supernumerary to start with. You're not in the numbers?"

"But there's still so much to do. So many women. And –" I pause. I don't want to say the words. I don't want Zoe to think that I'm not doing everything that I possibly can be, everything I should be. "I feel like I'm letting the women down. They deserve so much more."

Zoe stands beside me and strokes my hair away from my face.

"There's a lot going on, Vi," she says. "It's a big change, going from student to being a qualified staff member."

"You're feeling it too?" I say. Of course I don't want her to be going through anything like what I am, but knowing that she can relate might help me to feel a little bit better.

"Not like you, no. But the kids all know that I'm new, and some of them push it, trying to test me. Or, you know, just trying to push me."

I nod. She doesn't seem fazed by what she has told me. It's almost as though it was something that she expected and is taking in her stride.

"It's a transition period for both of us," she says. "Have you talked to your mentor about how you're feeling? You know I'm here for you, and you can chat with me any time, any time at all, but she's probably heard these kinds of worries from students before."

I must frown a little too sternly because Zoe says, "That doesn't mean that what you're feeling doesn't matter, or that you should accept it. I mean, well, I suppose I mean that settling in is tough. Other people must find it tough too."

I sigh and rest my head against her belly, letting her carry on stroking my hair. It's so soothing, knowing that she is here with me, knowing that she is here for me.

"I'll talk to Becky tomorrow," I say, sighing into Zoe's apron.

"I'm sure she can help," Zoe says. "But you know you can do this, right? These feelings are going to pass."

I hope so. I hope that I'm strong enough to keep going because midwifery has been my dream for as long as I can remember. If I can't do this, if I don't enjoy this, what is there for me?

I pull back and look up at Zoe's strong, smiling face as the front door clicks open, and Luke walks into the hallway.

# Chapter Seven

After the hectic pace of the past couple of days, the break between Wednesday's early shift and my late on Thursday is much needed. The evening with Zoe and Luke somehow helped me to gain some sense of perspective and balance. I settle into bed just before eleven. I've never been one for late nights, and now, more than ever, I feel like I need my sleep. Stupidly I think that sleep will give my brain time to disengage, and give me a break from overthinking and anxious thoughts.

When I wake up in a cold clammy sweat at three o'clock I realise how naïve that thought was. My heart is racing in a crazy, fluttered gallop. I don't remember the exact details of my nightmare, but I was at work, or at least in a hellish version of work. The ward was identical to the Margaret Beresford Unit, apart from one fact: the corridor was never-ending, with an infinite number of beds lining its sides. I was standing at the end of the ward, looking into the vastitude, while hollow-eyed, desperate women repeated the same phrase: *I don't want to waste your time.*

A powerful judder shakes my body as I think of those words. My fear wasn't about being on the unit, or having an impossibly immense number of women to care for, although that was part of it. The real chest-aching distress came from those words, just as it had on the ward.

I need to get this in hand. I can't do this to myself. I've had so many anxiety attacks over the past ten years that I should be able to handle them by now, but the truth is that every time one grabs me I flop around like a helpless ragdoll in its control. Now, more than ever, I feel useless, powerless, and stupid.

Think about something else. Focus. Breathe. Deep, slow, steady.

I mentally run through the steps that I always take, and that sometimes work. I focus on the heavy shuddering tension in my muscles and force each part of me in turn to relax into the bed. This helps me to relax physically, and by turning my attention to my physical sensations I am trying to distract my brain from its chaotic thoughts. I focus on my breathing, taking the long, deep inhalations, exhaling slowly, and trying to get my heart rate under control.

*I am safe. I am here, at home in my bed. I am warm. I am safe.*

I am flipping tired.

Three am. There's plenty of time for more sleep. I turn my mind to my plans for later in the morning, try to think about what I will do once I've shaken this and successfully managed to sleep.

I can set my alarm for ten, or eleven even, and I'll still be able to take a long bath, read some of my book and eat lunch in front of an episode of *Salvage Den*. Those little luxuries – because they are luxuries to me – are all part of my plans for the morning. It might not seem much, to be able to relax and do those simple things, but if I am going to get through the shifts where I'm on my feet for eight hours I'm going to have to perfect my self-care routine. Getting enough good quality sleep is one of the most important parts of that, and lying here, staring at the darkness of my room, waiting for my heart to stop thundering is not helping.

*Don't think about it. Don't think about it. Focus. Breathe.*

My internal voice speaks softly and calmly, and I listen. Gradually my body takes over, picking up the rhythm of my words. My muscles loosen, my mind gives up its fight against me, and my heart rate settles to a stable pace.

*Sleep. Sleep now. Sleep.*

Eventually, I do.

I'm bleary eyed and dazed when my alarm goes off at ten. The events of the night flash up in my head as I start to come to, but I know better than to let myself focus on them for too long. If I start to think about what my dreams mean I'll only cause myself to be dragged back into that anxious state. I expected this to happen. Not the nightmare, but the panic. I've been free from attacks for the most part over the past few months, but whenever I'm in a new, stressful situation my body always sinks back into its destructive patterns. Anticipating anxiety doesn't make it any easier to cope with.

I could stay in bed, and I'm tempted to pick up my book, lie here reading, and perhaps slip back into a doze until eleven, but I choose not to. I want that bath. I want to sink into warm, calming water and relax. That was my plan, and that is what I'm going to do. If I go now, I might be able to make it downstairs to *Bon Appétit* and get coffee and croissants for breakfast. I deserve a treat, that's for sure.

There's something else on my mind though. It's not just the anxiety of the past few days that's nipping away at my mind. There's something else.

Even though I was told that it can take a couple of weeks for my PIN to arrive, I've been checking the post every morning. I gave my change of address to the Nursing and Midwifery Council – the NMC – who are responsible for the register of nurses and midwives that I'm eagerly awaiting enrolment on. Or am I? Already I'm starting to doubt whether I want that number to arrive. Even though I am supernumerary now, I'm still able to carry out enough duties to keep me as busy as I have been over the past two days. What's it going to be like when I get my PIN and I have my own workload of women to care for?

Of course, I'll have Becky's support. I'm not going to be thrown in at the deep end as soon as my registration comes through. Preceptorship is designed to ease the transition period. If I can't cope, I can talk to her, which is exactly what I am going to do today. But first there's the matter of a hot bath and a cheeky breakfast in the deli below. I almost manage a smile as I pull myself up, out of bed, and make my way to the bathroom. If I keep taking care of myself maybe the smiles will come more easily. Maybe I can get through this.

My morning of relaxation passes all too quickly, and before I know it, it's time for work again. I can tell as soon as I walk onto the ward that things have eased. The atmosphere is calmer; there's no sign of anyone hurrying along the corridors as there has been for the past couple of days. When I reach the office and see two of the morning staff chatting casually with a paediatrician I'm almost overwhelmed with relief. We've barely had chance to sit to complete our paperwork since Monday, so being able to talk to each other is a positive and very welcome sign.

"Are you okay, love?" Sam asks.

I nod, wordlessly, and realise that once again my emotions are clear to read on my face. I've been working myself up into such a state about coming back here, and now, finding that all my worry was for nothing, I don't just feel relieved, I feel stupid.

"Come and sit down. You've got ten minutes yet," she says, patting the chair next to her.

I follow her suggestion and slide down onto the seat.

"You look a bit pale," she says, leaning in towards my face. "Not coming down with something, are you?"

"Uh, no," I say. "I didn't sleep very well. I'll be okay. Thanks."

It's only a half-lie. I'm ready to talk to Becky about my self-doubt and anxieties, but I'm not sure I can discuss my inner-most feelings with everyone on the ward.

She reaches out to feel my forehead, and then takes hold of my wrist, palpating my pulse as though I were one of the women under her care. I suppose in a way I am.

"Hmm," she says. "Seems okay. Don't want you going near all those babies if you're brewing a bug," she smiles.

I sigh, and decide to give a little bit more away.

"I only started here this week," I say. I'm talking to Sam, but the other midwife and the doctor are both listening too. I breathe, and continue. "It's been a bit, er, tough," I say, and then correct myself. "It's been really busy." I finish with a smile, hoping they'll see it as an observation rather than a complaint.

"That's how it is up here, pet," the other midwife says. "It's all or nothing."

I remember that from my days of being a student, but it didn't impact me in quite the same way then. Being a student midwife on postnatal ward didn't prepare me for the reality of working here. There are a lot of skills that I need to pick up – and quickly – if I'm going to get through this.

Sam nods in agreement.

"September is the worst though," she says. "Usually, anyway."

Nine months after Christmas, of course. Nine months ago, I was at home with Mum, spending my last festive break as a student midwife away from my boyfriend. I certainly wasn't doing anything that would land me in a maternity hospital as anything other than a member of staff. How things change over the course of a year. By the time this Christmas comes around Zoe and Luke will be married. How things change.

"Today is better anyway," Sam smiles. "Make the most of it while you can."

A quiet day will give me the chance to talk to Becky, and to do what I came here for: support women.

"I will," I say. The words come out more solemnly than I mean them too, and Sam nudges me and laughs.

"Chin up, love. It might never happen."

The other midwife and the paediatrician smile too, but there are kind looks of understanding on their faces, rather than mockery. Each of them has been a new starter at some point. I guess everyone has been. The women on the ward are experiencing their own new beginnings with their newborn babies. Even if these are their second, third, or sixth children, each new infant brings their own demands and delights.

"Okay ladies?"

It's Becky, standing in the doorway, watching the three of them smiling, and me, well, who knows what I look like? I straighten my expression, and then force myself to form a smile too.

"Hi," I say.

"Welcome to another wonderful day on the Margaret Beresford Unit," Sam says.

"Every day is a pleasure," Becky replies.

She takes a seat, and the conversation turns away from me, towards a TV programme that the others were watching last night. I haven't heard of it, but I'm pleased that I'm not the focus of their attention anymore. I do want – and need – support, but I don't want to feel like everyone has to keep their eye on me, like I'm some kind of fragile liability or something. I worked hard to be here, and I will work hard to consolidate my practice.

The shift continues as peacefully as it began. Becky and I stroll to our end of the ward, chat to our allocated women and check that everyone is okay. *Okay* varies from not struggling with breastfeeding the two-day old baby that wouldn't latch onto the breast yesterday to feeling comfortable despite sitting on a sutured perineum following a forceps delivery. There's a sliding scale of *okayness* amongst the women on the ward, but for now, everyone does seem to have achieved a suitable level. I guess it's the same for me. How am I feeling today? Decidedly *okay*. Able to breathe, clear-minded, and much less stressed than I have been recently. Was I really working myself up into such a state over a few busy days? It almost seems silly to talk to Becky and tell her that perhaps I'm not coping quite so well with my transition to being a qualified midwife when today I am absolutely *okay*. Not great, not amazing, but definitely okay.

We wheel the drugs trolley around the ward, casually chatting between ourselves on the long, empty stretch of corridor, and then talking to the women that we stop off by on the ward. A lot of this job involves making small talk. I'm not particularly good at this in my social life, but here it flows freely, and I slip into the same level of conversation while I'm talking to Becky as I do when nattering with the women. It's insubstantial, but I know that conversation means a lot to the people I am talking to, so it means a lot to me. Today nobody feels that they are wasting our time. Today we can sit beside a second-time mum and chat about how much she's enjoying being on the ward with us, but how much she's looking forward to getting home tomorrow.

"I just needed a break, you know," she confides, and we understand.

Today we can talk to the new mum who's having trouble breastfeeding, and not only show her how to position her baby for this feed, but we can give her suggestions of other ways, and explain the mechanics behind feeding. On busy days we can do our job. On more peaceful days, like this, we can give more. I wish it were always like this. This is easy – but this is how it should be.

Easy.

Not having to carry out all the duties that I will need to do when I get my PIN is easy.

I have a deep-lying inkling that I am not going to find it quite as easy when that time comes.

As I push the medicines trolley back up the ward and back to the clinical room, Becky carries on with the light chatter.

I nod and smile, and then, once we have secured the trolley back in place, I take a deep breath and begin.

“Do you think we could…I mean, is it okay if we…” There’s that old familiar heavy thumping in my chest. Faster and faster. Slow down; it’s only Becky.

“Are you alright?” she asks, reaching her hand out towards me and placing it on my forearm, as if to steady me, or perhaps ground me.

“Er, sort of. Yes, I’m alright, but…” My thoughts are all over the place and my words don’t want to come together. “Could we talk? Please?”

Becky leans back slightly and looks me over, as if assessing the situation in the way she would a patient.

“Sure,” she says. “Of course. Do you want to grab a cup of tea? We can go in the seminar room, there’s nothing happening today.”

I don’t think I’ve seen a single seminar taking place in the seminar room yet. Sometimes the senior midwives and doctors gather in there for various meetings, but it’s always a closed-door affair. As Becky says though, it’s empty and quiet. Much better we talk there rather than in the office. I don’t want to say what I want to say in front of everyone else.

Becky goes to drop some paperwork into the office, and I make the tea. I’m already starting to doubt my thoughts as I pour the water into the mugs and stir, stir, stir. I have to shake myself to attention when

I'm pouring the milk so that I don't overfill and let it spill over onto the dull institutional worktop. It will be fine, I tell myself. It's just Becky. I keep repeating the thought as I carry our drinks into the seminar room, and sit and wait for my mentor.

She's not long behind me.

"I wish we had biscuits," she says, with a smile. I can see the concern lingering on her face behind her expression though.

"I'm trying to be good," I reply. I can't carry on with the small talk now though. I need to get to my point before I bottle it.

"So, what's up?" Becky pushes me in the right direction.

"I feel silly," I say. "Today is lovely, you know. I'm enjoying being here. The women are all super. Everything is, well, it's great. If every day were like this…"

Becky is giving me her full attention, nodding as I speak, and I can already feel her warmth and empathy. It's only making me feel guilty about complaining. Is that what I'm doing?

"The past couple of days," I say, changing tack. "I've found them so hard. I don't want you to think that I don't love it here, or that I'm not enjoying it, or that I can't do it…"

I stop again.

"Is that what you think?" she asks.

"Wh-what?" I stutter.

"Are you having those doubts? That perhaps you don't love it here? Maybe you're not enjoying it as much as you thought you would?" She looks at me for a few seconds before asking, "Do you feel like you can't do this?"

It's my turn to be silent. I look at her, and then I look down at my hands, to the green logo-emblazoned mug that I'm holding. Anything other than eye-contact with Becky.

"Would it surprise you to know that some days *I* find it hard?" she asks, with the emphasis on the *'I'*. "I find it hard. All of us do, at some point. Long days, busy wards, demanding patients…"

I look at her, eyebrows raised at the words.

"Not demanding in the negative sense. Justifiably demanding. The women are here for our support and our care. They're supposed to make demands. Perhaps it's not the right word, but you know what I mean. Anyway. The general *demands* of the job, I suppose. That's what I'm getting at. Sometimes, it does feel too much."

I know Becky is trying to reassure me, and help me to understand that my feelings are normal, but the thought that I might always feel as overwhelmed and uncertain as I have the past few days is a harsh blow.

"I don't know if I can do it," I say. "You're right."

"I've worked with you a lot over the past few years, Violet. You are a competent, caring, compassionate woman. You were a good student, and you're going to be a great midwife."

I have to look away again. Praise is as hard for me to take as the difficult questions were.

"Violet."

I shake my head, and slowly turn my eyes back towards my mentor.

"I don't feel like I am," I say. "It's my first week here, and I'm already struggling. I've not even got my PIN yet."

"Maybe you will feel better when you have," Becky suggests. "You'll be in control of organising your time. I'll make sure you only have as much as you can handle, I promise."

"And what if it's like it has been the past couple of days?" I ask. I can hear a whine in my voice that I can't bear. I shouldn't be sitting here, complaining like this. I should be happy that I passed my course, that I qualified for my dream career, and that I landed this job. I hate my stupid, ungrateful attitude. I hate my inability to cope.

"Is it your anxiety that is making you feel this way, or is there something else?" Becky asks.

The question hits me hard, and I don't immediately know the answer. Am I anxious because I can't do it? Because it feels like too much? Or does it feel too much *because* I am anxious?

"It's…I don't know. It's hard to tell," I say.

"Give yourself a break," Becky says. "Alright? Try to, at least. How about you see how it goes over the next few shifts, and we can meet up and talk again, see if you're still feeling like this?"

Maybe every day will feel like today has felt. Maybe the past couple of days were the shock to my system that comes with starting out in a new role. Maybe this is normal, or at least normal for me.

"I'll do my best," I say.

"If I can do anything else for you over your next few shifts, you let me know, okay?"

I nod.

"Is there anything else I can do right now?"

"I don't think so," I tell her. "Being able to talk to you helps though. Thanks Becky."

I'm not sure how much it has helped, but at least I have a plan now. I can't beat myself up about not talking to anyone about how I feel either now that I have unburdened my worries onto Becky.

"When are your days off?" she asks. "Weekend, like me?"

"Yeah," I say. "Back on early shift Monday. I think we have the same off-duty while I settle in."

"That's good," she says. "Plan something nice for the weekend. Look after yourself, and talk to me any time. Alright?"

I nod again.
"Alright?" she repeats.
"Alright," I say.

I'm not completely certain if it's okay or not. I've always been able to talk to Becky. She was the first mentor that I told about my struggles with anxiety, and she confided that she has dealt with the same issues. I know I can rely on her, but I also know that I must rely on myself too. I have to learn how to cope with the busy days, because they might not come all the time, but they do, and they will.

# Chapter Eight

My plans for the weekend consist of a lie-in on Saturday morning, and then a trip into town with Zoe for brunch and shopping. Seeing as I'm used to waking at some time between six and six-thirty in the morning, my idea of a lie-in is waking up at eight o'clock. I've never been able to sleep much later than that, and since I've been conditioning my body to let me work early shifts over the past three years I'm now used to this. On the flip side it means that I never stay up much past eleven at night. I doubt I would turn into a pumpkin if I were to be found awake at midnight, but I can't remember the last time I made it to that time.

By ten past eight, my plan of reading a chapter of my book before I drag myself up is interrupted by my need to head to the bathroom, and once I'm up, I'm up.

It's been quite a week.

While I'm washing my hands, I look at the reflection of my pale, slightly spotty face in the mirror above the sink. My brown eyes are accessorised with dark circles. There's a pimple on my cheek and a light rash on my forehead. I can't help but frown as I stare at my imperfections. Did I look this bad a week ago, before I went back to the ward? A week ago, I was staying with Zoe and

Luke, getting excited/scared about moving in here. Only a week ago. I splash cold water over my dull skin and pat it dry, as much as to stop myself from looking as anything else.

Of course I had my doubts last week. I had my doubts about moving here. I had doubts about starting work. I had doubts that I could live on my own, that I could be a midwife, that I could be a fully functioning adult female. I had doubts because that's what I do. Perhaps Becky asked exactly the right question. Is it just my anxiety that's making me feel the way I am?

*Just* my anxiety.

The thought makes me actually laugh out loud. There's no such thing as 'just' my anxiety. It's been one of my defining features for so long that sometimes I think it affects everything I do. And then sometimes I'm in control of it, or at least in control of myself.

I tried medication, sure. When I was first diagnosed, and then again, a couple of years ago. Not for long though; probably not for long enough. I almost went to counselling. Almost. The waiting lists are long, and I always seem to find a way to talk myself out of going, or, like last time, someone else talks me out of it. My ex-boyfriend. I should never have let him get involved, but obviously *I* thought he was doing what *he* thought was best for me. Instead, he was preying upon my vulnerability.

I have been stupid, but I'm not anymore. At least I'm not quite so stupid now.

I'm trying to relax and have a happy weekend, I don't want to think about my anxiety, and I definitely don't want to think about *That Guy*.

Shopping with Zoe. More precisely bridal shopping with Zoe. That's what I should be focussing on. We love to shop, and what could be more exciting than shopping for your best friend's wedding. The thought makes my reflection crack a smile, and though my face looks weary and dishevelled, I feel the rush of happiness hit me.

"Zoe and Luke," I say. "Zoe and Luke."

Their names fit so well together as I speak the words, and saying them out loud is like a magic spell that fills my mind and stops me from thinking about anything negative.

I rub foundation onto my pasty skin, bring my eyes to life with mascara and pull a tropical coral lip gloss out of the bottom of my make-up bag to finish the look.

The make-up and the mantra might just be cover-ups, concealing what is going on beneath, but today that's what I need.

Even though Zoe drives, we both live close enough to the town centre that it's more convenient to walk to our meeting point rather than go by car. Having lived together for the past three years, spending most of the week without seeing her has been a strange experience. I stand in the street outside the department store that we've decided to wander around first, waiting for her to arrive. The Square is busy for this time of the day, mostly women and children, some combinations of these, and the occasional couple, wrapped up in each other, smiling, happy. That's what I see from the outside anyway. Who knows what's going on in their lives or inside their minds? Would any of them imagine the way that my mind is ticking over with anxious energy while I stand here waiting for Zo? I should have brought a novel and sat on one of the benches, or brought my headphones so that I could listen to music or an audiobook. The last thing I need right now is time to think.

"Violet! Hey!"

The sound comes from my left. I'd been looking out across the square, expecting her to head the way we always come down into town, but things have changed. She lives in the opposite direction now; how could I have forgotten?

I catch my breath, and unable to think quickly enough before I act, I throw my arms out towards Zoe and catch her in a mighty embrace.

"Alright, alright!" she laughs.

"Oh, it's so good to see you," I tell my best friend.

"You too, Vi." Her cheek is warm against mine as she presses into me, no more willing to break away from the hug than I am.

I resolve here and now that I'm not going to moan on about my work issues today. I want to spend time with Zoe, enjoy myself and talk about happier things. That's going to be made a lot easier by the fact that today we are shopping for one of the most important wedding essentials – her dress. By default, that means we'll be looking for a bridesmaid gown for me as well, but I'm far more excited about helping Zoe to find the dress of her dreams. Not too flouncy, not too sleek, and definitely no mermaid tail.

There aren't many shops left on Cranbourne High Street. We have three department stores and a smattering of clothing chain stores, but the big names have left the town centre in favour of a satellite shopping centre out by the motorway. What we do have - in spades - are coffee shops.

"Beecher's first and then brunch?" Zoe suggests.

I turn my head to the looming department store behind us. We may only have those three department stores, but Beecher's, the largest of them, is a five-floor behemoth of a building. I'm definitely going to need brunch after we've finished in there.

"I'll follow you," I say. "You're the bride."

She grins. "To be honest, I want to try dresses on before I stuff my face at *Coffee Express*," she says.

Trying on dresses makes everything feel so much more real and immediate. I know that Zoe and Luke are engaged and living together, but I still can't imagine the two of them as husband and wife. It seems surreal, in the same way that imagining myself as a registered midwife does.

I push the thought out of my mind, and link arms with Zoe.

"Let's go and find the dress of your dreams," I say.

Her face expands into a blissfully happy smile, and suddenly all I can think about is Zoe and Luke, Zoe and Luke, Zoe and Luke.

The dress department is on the top floor, tucked away in the far corner behind the travel bags and suitcases. At the entrance is a mannequin bedecked in a huge meringue of a dress: satin bodice with training ribbons and a full skirt like a ballgown.

"I'm not sure what I'm looking for," Zoe says, "but I think it's the opposite of that."

I laugh, too loudly, and the lady behind the counter shoots a sharp look in my direction.

"Uh-oh," I say in a hushed tone. "Look what I've done."

The woman, sharply dressed in a black pencil skirt and white shirt with a waistcoat on top, strides over in our direction.

Zoe instinctively straightens herself up, and I close my lips together firmly. This is Zoe's day; I mustn't say or do anything stupid. Not now.

"Ladies," the woman says, looking from Zoe to me and back again. "Can I help you?"

"We're just looking," Zoe says.

The woman takes a quick snorting intake of breath.

"Which one of you is planning for your big day?" she says in a voice that sounds rehearsed and forced.

I'm sure she must have asked this question countless times before, and I wonder if I ever sound like this to my patients. We repeat ourselves so frequently on the ward that I'm sure there's a danger of our tones becoming robotic. *When did you last feel baby move? How often are your contractions? How long are they lasting? Have you passed urine recently?* Of course the bridal sales assistant doesn't ask any of those things.

Zoe raises her hand, like one of the kids in her classroom.

"Very well." The assistant is almost literally looking down her nose at Zoe, peering over a green-rimmed pair of almond-shaped glasses. "And what are you looking for?"

"I'm don't know yet," Zoe says. "Like I said, we're just looking."

"Have you any ideas?"

The woman breaks eye contact, looking from rack to rack, as if trying to locate a dress that she can recommend to her potential customer.

"I've seen some things on the internet that I like. I wanted to have a look around, maybe try some things on?"

The assistant's eyes snap to Zoe's hands, and I realise immediately that she's checking for signs of sticky fingers that might mark the merchandise. I almost laugh, but instead I keep my mouth shut.

"Is that okay?" Zoe asks.

"Let me help you," the woman persists. "Do you have any images with you, of shapes or necklines? Do you want satin or crepe? Lace or no lace? Mermaid, ballgown, A-line? Full length, midi, tea-length?"

Tea and crepes sound amazing around now, and I'm already wishing that we had gone for brunch first.

"You're going to have to slow down," Zoe says patiently. She starts to fumble in her bag, looking for her phone.

"Come, come," the woman ushers the two of us over to a large velvet sofa, and invites us to sit. "Let me have a look at your photos, and we'll take it from there."

It feels like we are completely out of our depth, in a new world with a specialist who knows all the technical jargon, the ins and outs and workings of every detail, while we are flapping around, clueless. Again, I can't help but think that this is how the new mums must feel when they are thrown in at the deep end on the wards. Everything is new and confusing, and there's so much to take in.

Zoe clicks her phone screen and opens the Pinterest app, where she has saved all her wedding ideas on various neatly curated boards. There's one for venue, one for flowers, one for cakes (that's my favourite), several others dedicated to the most intricate details, and, of course, one for dresses. She turns the phone around towards the woman, who sits next to her, and waits as the assistant runs her finger over the screen, peering in turn at each of her ideas.

"There are a lot of different styles here," the woman sighs. "Different fabrics, different cuts." She looks up at Zoe. "Perhaps you could point out which elements of each dress you would like. It might not be possible to find exactly what you want. To have a dress designed completely to your specification would cost, well…" She leans back slightly and looks over her glasses again. "What exactly *is* your budget?" she asks.

This must be how I look when I'm reading through a birth plan, or telling someone '*of course you can breastfeed, but…*'.

Zoe bites her lip, and looks at the assistant. "I have an idea in mind, but I could spend a little more on the right dress," she says.

We've talked about this. In our previous conversation Zoe said that she didn't want to come out with a number because she was worried that she'd only be offered expensive dresses at the top end of her price range if she named her budget. Zoe and Luke have both just started work, and although they have decent jobs, neither of them is loaded. Luke has some savings, and Zoe's parents are chipping in, but I know already that they are going to be aiming for a beautiful but not-particularly expensive wedding. I'm buying my own bridesmaid dress because I insisted on it.

The assistant sighs again and spins the phone back towards Zoe. "I can't help you if I don't know what to show you," she says.

This is definitely not how I come across to my patients, I'm fairly sure of that now. Her impatience is making me feel uncomfortable, so I can't imagine how Zoe must be feeling. She's remarkable calm, despite the attitude of the assistant.

"Less than five hundred pounds, then," Zoe says.

I jump a little at the figure. I thought she was aiming for even less than that. It seems like an awful lot for a dress that she will only get to wear once. If I ever get married I'll probably pick up a second-hand number from Oxfam, and get Zoe to do my hair and make-up. Not that it will ever happen.

"We have a few dresses in your price range," the assistant says.

"I don't want anything too long," Zoe says. "And I want sleeves. Lace sleeves. Nothing too, er, flouncy, you know. Maybe A-line, certainly not like that." She gestures towards the mannequin." She's on a roll now she's started talking. Saying the magic number has given her the confidence, it seems. "Cream, not white. I'm pale enough," she smiles.

The assistant doesn't return the smile, but she nods, softening. Now that Zoe is talking, perhaps it's making her job easier.

"A mid-length would suit your height," she says. Zoe's petite figure was not built for long dresses, and she seldom wears them.

"Cream, yes. Perfect for your red hair and freckles." She stands up, and pulls on Zoe's hand, bringing her to her feet too. Looking Zoe up and down, she moves her hand in a quick gesture, encouraging Zoe to circle around. "Yes, yes," she says, as though an image is becoming clear in her mind.

"Maybe beaded," Zoe says, shrugging. "I'm not sure."

"Let's pull out a few, and you can try on the ones that you like."

The woman hurries off towards the racks and starts to flick through, leaving Zoe standing in front of me.

"Okay," I say. "That went, er, okay?"

"As soon as she thought I was genuinely going to spend some money, sure." Zoe smiles at me, and flops back on the sofa beside me. "My little heart was all fluttery, and not with the excitement of the wedding."

I smile back. "Do you really want to spend that much?" I ask.

She gives me a tiny shrug. "I want to try on some nice dresses, and see what's out there. If I end up getting something cheaper later down the line, that's fine. I feel like dressing up and feeling like a princess today. I don't think she would have let me try on *anything* if I said that I want to spend three hundred tops."

"True," I say with a tight-lipped grin. "She's not the kind to be messed with."

"This is all part of the fun, right?" she says. "Trying on the dresses is part of the experience of getting married. I *want* to try things that I can't afford. I want to look beautiful."

"You always do!" I say. "You could get married in your jeans and a jumper and Luke wouldn't care. You'd still look wonderful."

She nudges me in the ribs. "Thanks Vi, but I want to *know* that I look wonderful. Just for that one day."

I shake my head. I'm secretly looking forward to wearing my bridesmaid's gown too.  I'm usually either clad in my uniform or lounging around in a dress, tights and pumps. We get excited about the simple things, but on the flip side of that it means that the simple, uncomplicated things please us. Neither of us have ever needed much to be happy. Especially when we have always had each other. Whatever dress Zoe buys, she will be the most beautiful bride. Whatever happens, she will always be my best friend.

"You will," I tell her. "It's going to be amazing."

# Chapter Nine

Monday morning, I awake refreshed and revitalised. I've had all weekend to reflect and recover – and to remind myself of two important facts. Number one: midwifery is my dream job. Number two: I've worked my backside off to get where I am today. There is a list of other factoids that I've added into the mantra that I chant as I open my eyes, stretch, and prepare to face the day. I can do this. I am good enough. Blah blah blah. They're the same things I've been telling myself for years. I try to make my anxious brain believe the things that my rational brain already knows. I've decided to focus on the indisputable facts. Even anxiety can't make me disbelieve the truth.

Midwifery is my dream job.

I've worked my backside off to get where I am today.

I have a short but important itinerary to run through this morning, before my shift later today. Menial, dull household chores that I will get out of the way first, and then a long-overdue phone call to my mum. That's not something that I have to 'get out of the way'. Mum and I have a close relationship. Even though I moved out of home to go to uni and never went back, I have the luxury of knowing that she is less than an hour away, even by bus. I chose the closest university to my childhood home; Zoe and I both did. Family, home, and friendship; that's what we're all about. It figures that I'd become a midwife and she would be a teacher. It's almost as though those career paths were mapped out for us. They were the obvious choices.

I've lived in this flat for a whole week, but I can't say that it's starting to feel like home yet. I don't have a lot of personal possessions. I moved from my student residence to a stopgap stay with Zoe and Luke and straight into this place. I own clothes and books and, well, not a lot else. I need to start personalising my living space: some blankets, fairy lights, all the cosy details that will make me start to believe that I really live here, that this is really *me*. If I have time after my call to Mum I'll pop into town and see if I can get some starter items. I'm not going to rush though. I'm not rushing anything today.

My feet hit the floor, and I slide them into my fluffy grey slippers. I wear pyjamas, even though I live alone, because I feel the cold, and if I slept naked I'd no doubt wake up at two in the morning and have to pull on some kind of sleepwear. Even when I had a boyfriend who lived in the same house as I did, I spent most of my nights alone. I fidget, and Zoe has told me several times that I talk in my sleep. I've awoken a handful of times to find her sitting on the edge of my bed, resting a hand upon my back, trying to soothe me after I've shouted my way through a bad dream. It's not that I don't like cuddling up to someone, but I enjoy my own space too. I don't like being lonely, but sometimes I like to be on my own.

This morning I have time to think about all of these things because I am not – I am definitely, decidedly not – worrying about my upcoming shift. Or at least I'm not worrying when I get out of bed. I'm not worrying when I walk into the kitchen, smile at my own face in the mirror, brush my teeth and give my face the once-over. I'm not worrying until I walk out into the hallway and see the envelope that's waiting on the doormat.

"Welcome!" the mat declares in a bold, funky rainbow print.

I already know, before I bend my knees and squat on the floor next to the seemingly innocent oblong paper rectangle, that this letter is not at all welcome.

It's face-down. I could be wrong. It might not be what I think it is.

As I pick it up and flip it over to see my name and this address in the small transparent window, I know. Emblazoned across the bottom corner of the envelope are those letters: NMC. There's no getting away from it. This is my PIN. This changes everything.

I don't open the envelope straight away. I carry it through to the kitchen and put it down on the table, propped up against the wall so that I can sit and look at it as I stir my Ready Brek with languid indifference. I sip my tea and look at the envelope. I bring the spoon to my mouth and look at the envelope. My heart taps out a rhythm that's too fast and too fierce for a fit and healthy young woman who's simply sitting at her dining table – and I look at the envelope.

After everything I went through to get here… *(Midwifery is my dream job. I've worked my backside off to get where I am today.)* I can barely believe how intimidating I am finding the thought of opening the envelope and taking the next step forward into my career. I know that my PIN is within that paper receptacle. It's not as though this is a Schrödinger's cat type of situation. Whether I open that envelope or not, my cat is well and truly alive – or should that be dead? Whether or not I open it, my PIN is inside. I'm on the nursing and midwifery register, an official staff member.

I suddenly feel a deep pang of regret that I haven't kept in contact with the other students from my course. We've not shared a single message since the first days after we finished. One of my cohort applied for a job at St. Jude's, but in the short space of time between his interview and what would have been his start date, he decided to make a move to one of the big London hospitals instead. Again, I feel alone. I could send a message to the group chat we had going during our course. Everyone is still linked in; maybe I could start a conversation. My social ineptitude is almost as strong as my self-doubt. I am going to have to really push myself if I want to get in touch with the uni gang.

"You're pathetic," I tell myself, and I hear the words in my father's voice. It's almost enough to make me slam down my spoon and leave the table, leave the letter, and…what? Where could I go? How can I run away from the truth?

"I am pathetic," I say again, shaking my head and reaching out for the envelope. Opening it won't change anything. What it will do is make me face up to the fact that I have to adjust. I have to adapt. I have to start believing in myself and stop being so pathetic.

Pathetic.

At work, as a student midwife, and as a qualified, pre-registration midwife, I have been sympathetic, and I have been empathetic. Pathos. Caring. It's what I do. It's one of the absolutely necessary personal characteristics required for anyone in the nursing and midwifery professions. Maybe being pathetic isn't such a bad thing. The original roots of the word are in an Ancient Greek word meaning something like being capable of feeling. It's only over time that the meaning has become corrupted and negative. I'm sensitive. I'm emotional. Sometimes that's a good thing, but right now I have to get it under control or it's going to be negative too.

"Yes," I tell myself as I pick up the envelope and start to tear it open. "I care. I'm a midwife. I'm supposed to care."

The envelope opens like a gaping mouth, the ripped paper on either side of the jagged tear like teeth, threatening to bite down on my fingers as I reach in for the letter.

"And I need to get a grip."

I hope that living alone isn't going to result in me having too many conversations with myself. It's bad enough that I talk in my sleep without chatting away to myself while I'm awake too.

*Midwifery is my dream job.*

*I've worked my backside off to get where I am today.*

There it is. Exactly what I expected. The A4 paper bears the NMC letterhead and, attached at the bottom by a smudge of some kind of peelable adhesive, is a laminated card that bears the magical digits of my registration number. I am registered. I have a PIN.

My stomach heaves, and I'm not certain whether it's due to fear or excitement. I drop the paper onto the table and race through to the bathroom, just making it to the toilet before I bring back what I've eaten of my breakfast.

I wipe my mouth, clean my teeth, and wipe the vomit-induced tears from my eyes.

"Well," I say to the mirror. "This is it."

Doing my chores is the last thing on my mind now. The household trivialities can wait. I'm in no mood to empty the dishwasher or decant the contents of the laundry hamper into the washing machine. I can see its reflection in the corner of the bathroom mirror, and I have to look away.

"Get it together," I tell myself as I walk back into the living room.

*Dream job. Whatever.*

As much as I would love to spend the morning talking to myself, alternating between panic and self-doubt, I sit on the sofa and address the other task on my to-do list. I phone my mum.

It's something I should probably do a lot more frequently than I actually do. When I first moved away I would phone and text regularly, but as time has gone on I've slacked. Even though she lives so close by I rarely visit. Now that I have my own place, perhaps I should invite her to visit me.

I can smell my minty breath bouncing back off my phone screen as I wait for her to answer the call.

"Pathetic," I tell myself. "Pathetic."

Mum answers with her usual cheery greeting, and it brings an instant smile to my face.

The first part of our call is always the same: the usual pleasantries and inquisition about whether I'm eating alright, sleeping well, and getting enough sunshine. The last of those enquiries has been a recent thing. She was horrified when I told her that sometimes I go to work before the sun has risen and come home after it has set. I daren't tell her about the night shifts where I've been on duty from half past nine at night until eight in the morning, returned home and slept all day until I had to get up, shower and leave for work again. As a student, those days were few and far between. As a qualified midwife, as a registered midwife now, I'll be expected to work a batch of night shifts each month.

"Are you still there, Violet?"

I could at least try to concentrate on the conversation rather than letting my mind wander.

"I'm here, Mum. Sorry."

"Must be a bad line," she says. "Anyway. How's Zoe? All excited for the wedding?"

Zoe has spent so much time with Mum and me over the years I'm sure that my mum thinks of her as a second daughter. At least Zoe seems to have her life together, which is more than can be said about me.

"Of course," I say, smiling at the thought of our shopping day. "She's got her heart set on a dress we found over the weekend, and they've picked out another venue they like, so it looks like it's all going to plan."

"Send her my love," Mum says.

"Will do," I say, as I always do, and then there's a palpable pause in our chatter.

"What's on your mind?" Mum's voice is tentative, but warm.

I don't reply straight away because I don't know what to say. I don't know how to talk about my fears without making her worried, and that's the last thing I want.

I sigh and speak.

"I got my PIN in the post today. You know, my registration number. I'm officially a registered midwife now."

"Well, that's wonderful," she says. "Isn't it?"

Again, I sigh.

"It's a big step," I tell her. "Massive. It feels enormous."

I can almost picture the expression on her face. She has a certain way of looking at me when I, infrequently, share my feelings with her. A kind of concerned caring sparkles in her eyes and grabs me deep in my chest. I can't see that over the phone, but I can feel it.

"It is," she agrees, calmly. "You've done so well, Violet. I'm so proud of you. I wish I had done something worthwhile in my life like you're doing."

"Worthwhile?" I repeat the word as a question. "Everything you do is worthwhile. You created me, cared for me, you still do. You still care for me, even though I'm not there to steal your biscuits and leave my clothes on the bathroom floor."

"I work in a shop. You're helping women to have babies." She says the words in a flat tone that reveals a lot more about her thoughts regarding her life choices.

I don't correct her to tell her that midwifery is so much more than that. How could I?

"It's so hard sometimes," I tell her.

"Of course, it is," she says. "Most important things are. If it were easy, if anyone could do it then there would be a lot more people clamouring for your job. Did you ever think it *would* be easy?" she asks.

"No," I say, quietly. Then I repeat the word, with certainty in my voice. "No."

"You knew the training was going to be tough, and you got through it."

"Yes."

"I wish I could say something to make you feel more confident, Violet. I wish that was the one thing you could have inherited from your stupid, over-confident and otherwise useless father."

I have to let out a little laugh at that. It's rare that I hear her mention anything positive about Dad since he left us.

"I don't know what to tell you though," she concludes.

"That's okay, Mum," I say. "Just talking to you helps."

"Come down and see me as soon as you can."

She always offers the invitation, and I always say that I will, but in truth I don't expect to be visiting before Christmas. I reply with a guilty "I miss you".

"You too," she says. "You too."

There are no easy answers. Mum didn't have the right words to say to me because there are no *right words*. My plans for the day have all gone out of the window, and all that remains is for me to pull my navy-blue uniform out of the wardrobe and start to get ready for my first day as a registered midwife.

I place the uniform, still on its hanger, onto my bed and look at it for a few seconds. It represents so much, and it fills me with so many mixed emotions. I can't let myself panic to the point of throwing up again, but as I let myself think, the nausea begins to rise.

*Look away. Get ready. Have a shower. Think positive thoughts.*

I can't quite bring myself to think those positive thoughts, but I do try not to think about anything negative as I shower and dry myself off. I know that some people have their most inspiring thoughts in the shower, but not me. Today, I try not to have any thoughts beyond which shower gel to use. I opt for vanilla, to find it reminds me of warm custard and sweet cakes, of Mum, of my home with her, of an easier, simple life.

When I had that simple life, I dreamed of this. The day that I would put on a midwife's uniform, and proudly walk onto a ward as a qualified member of staff. In my imagination, I had a wide smile, and strode with my head held high. In reality, I fumble to put my arms through the sleeve holes. I let go of the zip three times before I manage to grasp hold of it and pull it straight up the front of my tunic. How did I manage to feel so proud in the light blue top that I wore last week? Where is that feeling now? All I have is fear and flatness, and the feeling that I am about to fail.

Is that what it is? I'm not afraid of getting out there onto the ward, I'm afraid of failing. I'm afraid of letting women down. I'm afraid of letting my colleagues down. I'm afraid of letting Zoe, Mum, anyone who knows me down.

I'm afraid of letting myself down.

I force myself to bring my eyes up to the dressing table mirror and look at my uniformed reflection.

*Midwifery is my dream job.*

*I've worked my backside off to get where I am today.*

I say the words out loud, speaking to the average looking, averagely minded, anxious girl in the mirror.

My voice is shaking, and that nausea is still simmering inside of me. I can't let them down, and I can't let myself down. I know that however I feel, I have to get to work, and I have to do my best.

That's really all I can do.

# Chapter Ten

Anxiety aside, as I expected, I feel a dramatic difference walking onto the ward wearing my navy uniform. The letter and PIN registration card are in my bag, but Becky doesn't need to see them to know that they have arrived. The uniform tells her everything she needs to know.

"Ooh, exciting!" she exclaims, giving me a gentle hug as I enter the office.

"Terrifying," I smile, acknowledging my feelings and playing them down at the same time.

Becky laughs, and pulls me in towards her.

"I'm here, okay. You're going to be just fine."

The words should make me feel better, but inside I'm trembling, and trying not to let my actual fears show.

She pauses to look at me.

"Violet," she says. "I know this is tough, okay? It was the same for me. Believe me, I know. I'm not going to let anything bad happen to you." The first words that spring into my mind are, *'What happens if I do something bad?'*

I don't say that. Instead I nod, and thank her.

"Special treat," she says. "I'll make the tea today. Go and give yourself a few minutes to settle before we get going."

"Thanks," I smile. "Is it…is it busy?" I almost don't want to ask.

"It's decidedly average," she replies.

Average is perfect. I don't think I could cope with busy today, but I know that I have to get stuck in. I have to keep my mind and body occupied so that I don't spend the entire shift in a trembling mass of panic.

"Sounds great, I tell her."

Becky pats me gently on the arm, and goes to the kitchen. I hover in the corridor, catching my breath before I make my way into the office.

There's a tap on my shoulder, and I immediately assume that it's one of the women, about to ask me something before I've even had handover. It's fine, but I don't know anything about any of the patients that have come in over the weekend, and I'm not in the right mindset to be taken off-guard.

I turn to see a blonde midwife, her hair short-bobbed and curly, bouncing on the shoulders of her navy uniform. I don't recognise her, but she's wearing the same tunic as I am.

"Hi, I'm Beth," she says, pointing at her name badge.

"Violet," I say, uncertain whether I should shake hands. It feels too formal, but by the time my brain has caught up with my body, I've wobbled my hand tentatively towards her, not quite enough to be an offer, but too far to be a natural movement. I catch myself, and thrust it out, almost punching her in the process.

She laughs and takes my hand, shaking it daintily.

"Nice to meet you. Could you show me where to leave my bag?" she says. "First day here," she adds, by way of an explanation.

I realise I'm still holding her hand, and let go with a jump.

"I'm so sorry," I say. I'm making a complete idiot of myself, as I usually do when I meet someone new. "Come on, I'll show you."

The locker room is only a few doors along the corridor, but I'm in such a dither today I was afraid I'd give the wrong directions and end up sending Beth to the sluice room. Not such a great way to make friends or welcome someone new to the ward.

I push the door open and hold it for her, showing her inside.

"Use whichever you like," I tell her. "If it's locked it means…well, you're not daft, I'm sorry."

"Right," she says with a bemused smile. "I'll work it out. Thanks."

"We have handover in the room that I was standing outside."

She nods. "I'll throw my bag in and follow you," she says, quickly locating the nearest vacant space and doing just that. "Okay then."

She turns, and walks back towards me, and I remember to get out of the doorway to let her through.

Beth has a northern accent, from what I can tell, not much unlike Luke's Yorkshire twang. Something about it feels warm and familiar.

I had expected everyone's interest to be focussed on my navy uniform today, and I'm actually rather pleased when the midwives in the office turn their attention to the new girl instead. I say *girl* but Beth is probably around the same age as I am. Early twenties. Women, not girls - although sometimes I feel a lot more like a girl than a woman.

She takes a seat next to one of the morning staff and immediately everyone starts to make their introductions, recognising her, as I did, as one of our own. That's what this blue uniform does – it's not just something to be afraid of, it's a mark of belonging. We are a team, and we wear team colours. Despite my stuttering nerves I have a warm and pleasant feeling of being part of something.

There's a fourth midwife, a senior named Holly, on duty this afternoon as well as Becky, Beth, and I, which means that even if we did happen to have a full ward the workload would still be manageable. This rarely happens. There are usually three midwives, and two support workers at the very most. Because there was no way of knowing when my PIN would arrive, I've not been counted in the numbers for this week's shifts, so I'm going to have a little more time to settle in. I feel like I'm going to need it.

No one is singling me out for attention. They aren't cooing over my navy tunic. I'm blending in, fitting in, and that suits me perfectly.

Handover is short and simple. There were two elective Caesarean sections this morning, and the women are in side rooms, both absolutely fine. The third side room is occupied by the mother who gave birth to triplets last week. I'm going to be looking after one of the women who had her operative delivery this morning, and two other ladies who are out on the Nightingale ward down the same end that Becky is working. Three women and their babies should be a breeze: exactly what I need to ease me into my days as a navy-uniform wearing midwife.

"I'm sure you're going to be fine," Becky tells me, "but if you need anything at all, come and ask, okay?"

"Yep," I say, with an air of confidence that I didn't expect. "Thanks, Becky."

She gives me an encouraging thumbs-up and we set about our rounds. Holly tells the morning staff that they can leave early, there's not much else for them to do now that we have taken over. She and Beth set off towards their patients at the other end of the ward.

If every day could be like this – like it was on my first shift last week – I would feel a lot more confident. The busier the ward the more overwhelmed I get, but I don't think that can be unique to me.

During handover I was careful to make detailed notes about all of the women on the ward, because I didn't know then which women I would be allocated to look after. My sheet of A4 paper is scribbled all over with details from babies' last feeding times to who needs which blood tests and when.

The woman who had her Caesarean this morning is called Jessie Bloom, and I know that I am going to pop in to visit her first. She'll need four-hourly observations due to the fact that a C-section is actually classed as a major surgical procedure. I may not be a trained nurse, I went straight into my midwifery training from college, but I'll be putting my nursing skills to use today.

I pause outside the door to Jessie's side room and check through the notes I made during handover. Elective Caesarean for breech at thirty-nine weeks. First baby. Male infant. Breastfeeding. Beside that I drew a little line to add more detail in the margin: "needs to feed". It's two o'clock now. She delivered at eleven this morning (11:08, my notes say) so there's no panic yet. Her Caesarean was straightforward, and all observations have been within normal ranges so far. I try to retain the information, reading it again, and then repeating it in my head. I know I can look at the notes that are tucked neatly away in the blue plastic holder at the end of her bed, or I can pull this sheet of paper from my pocket again, but it would be great if I could just look like I know what I'm doing. I want to make a professional impression. After all, I'm a registered professional now, and she is my first patient.

Patient. I still feel uncomfortable using that word.

Before I tap on the door, I look through the small square of glass to see whether she is awake and alone. It's the start of visiting time, but as she came up from theatre this morning her birth partner could still be with her anyway.

She's propped up in bed, resting against her pillows, looking over at her sleeping baby. I can't help but smile; I'd probably be doing exactly the same as she is.

I keep the smile on my face, knock on the door lightly, and enter.

"Hi Jessie," I say. "I'm Violet. I'm one of the midwives on duty this afternoon, and I'll be looking after you."

I've said the words so many times before, but always with 'student' as part of the sentence. It almost feels as though I have missed something now that I am omitting the unnecessary word that is no longer part of my title.

“Hi,” she replies.

I cast my eyes over her, without making it obvious that I’m doing so. She looks tired, but well, and again I expect that I would be the same. There’s a bag of intravenous fluid running into a cannula in her left hand, and a blood pressure machine to her right side. Her catheter bag is clipped to a hooked stand on the bed just below the monitor, and it doesn’t look like it needs to be emptied yet.

“How are you feeling?” I ask. My anxious mind is telling me to pick up her notes, run through the checklist, carry out the observations, but my compassionate side reminds it that the most important place to start is with this: how are you feeling.

“Like someone has done the washing up in my belly,” she laughs. I’ve heard similar descriptions before, but I smile along with her.

“Any pain?”

She shakes her head. “No. Not yet.”

It’s nearly time for the drugs round, but her chart tells me that she had analgesia while she was in the recovery room, and she’s not due anything else for the time being.

“You’re written up for a couple of different types of pain relief,” I tell her. “Let me know as soon as you feel uncomfortable.”

The last thing either of us need is for her to wait until she's in roaring agony before she has analgesia. No point being brave. It's a major operation, and major operations lead to post-op pain.

"How's the little fellow?"

The baby is wrapped in a light blue waffle knit blanket inside the Perspex cot. His little perfectly rounded head pops out above the covers. I lean over and look at him.

"Isaac," she says, with a proud smile. "I haven't seen much of him yet. I'm sure he's fine, but he had a little suckle down in recovery and since then he's been asleep."

I turn to look at her instead, and nod reassuringly. "He should wake up for a feed when he's ready. If I'm not here, do buzz me, okay?"

"I was wondering what I was supposed to do," she says. "I don't think I could move to pick him up just yet."

"No, no," I tell her.

I run through the routine checks, chatting away to her as I do so, and everything appears to be absolutely fine. Of course, I'm pleased for Jessie that she's comfortable and happy, but I'm also relieved that my first day is starting off in the right direction.

"So, give me a buzz," I say. "Anything at all. I'll pop back in to see you soon, okay?"

She nods, and smiles, and I leave the room feeling positive.

The other two women that I am caring for today are both sitting up and chatting to their visitors as I walk down towards the end of the ward. Aisling, a new mum who had a normal delivery overnight, is dressed in pale blue pyjamas and fluffy pink slippers, sitting on top of her covers. The man that she's chatting to is holding the baby in his arms, unable to keep his eyes off the child. I'm guessing that he's the father, but I've learned not to make assumptions.

Across from Aisling is my other patient, Talia. The little girl in the cot beside her is her second baby. The two of them came up to the ward about an hour before our shift began, following a normal delivery with a mild postpartum haemorrhage. It's normal to have *some* blood loss at delivery, but anything over five hundred millilitres is considered a PPH – or postpartum haemorrhage. I know that I need to keep a close eye on her blood loss now, make sure it's not too heavy, and monitor her vital signs every four hours.

The rhythm to the day will be set by the observations that I need to carry out to make sure Aisling and Jessie are stable and comfortable. Although I want to spend my time supporting the women, getting to know them, and making sure they have as positive an experience as possible, I'm already using the required physical monitoring as a mental framework to plan my shift around. Observations, drug round, mealtimes, baby feeding; the necessities underlie my care planning. This is how I will organise my time, and this is how I'll stay focused and remain calm. Everything will be straightforward if I get the basics right. Now that I am moving around the ward, talking to the women, doing my job, I feel so much better.

As I sit beside Aisling and talk to her Becky walks down the corridor, passes by us and smiles. The smile that I return to her is easy and comfortable. I am doing this. I'm fine.

# Chapter Eleven

I keep to the rhythm that the observations dictate, chatting to the ladies, and then head back to the office to write in their postnatal care plans. At the end of the notes I sign my name *Violet Cobham, Registered Midwife* for the very first time and can't help but pause and stare at the paper in front of me.

"Feels good, doesn't it?" Beth says as she sees what I'm doing.

I look down at my navy tunic, and then look back to the midwife.

"I can't quite believe it yet," I reply. "It's all a bit surreal."

She nods in understanding. "I know that feeling," she says.

"Are you okay?" I ask, remembering that it's her first day here. "Have you found everything you need?"

"Holly showed me around," Beth says. "And I've only walked into the linen cupboard instead of the side room three times so far, so…"

We both laugh, and I honestly can't believe how relaxed I feel.

Perhaps I just needed to get my PIN and get on with it. Now that I am thinking for myself, making decisions and organising my day everything seems to be falling into place. I have Becky, Beth, and Holly for support if I should happen to need them. I almost wonder what it was that I was so worried about, but my anxiety has been a part of me for so long that I already know. The real trick is in feeling that fear and doing it anyway, isn't that what they say?

It isn't long before I do have to reach out for that support.

After I finish completing the care plans I make my way back down to Jessie's room to help her to get baby Isaac to feed.

It's something that I've done so many times before. As a student I prided myself on my ability to support a woman to breastfeed. When Geri was my mentor she loved to throw me in at the deep end, and one of the things she encouraged me to do was to practise as much as possible. I found out early on with Geri that going to the office to tell her that one of the women needed help latching a baby to the breast would result in her telling me to *'go and do it then'*. Her special brand of tough love forced me to develop my skills, and I know that it has helped me so much to be the midwife I am today. Of course, when I am finally allocated students I will no doubt sit beside them and walk them through everything, but that's just who I am. We do things differently, but at the end of the day our role is to support women – and to support other midwives.

Isaac is red-faced and agitated, making the familiar sounds of a hungry newborn.

"Don't worry," I tell Jessie. "Let me help you to get into a comfortable position, and we'll have him feeding in no time."

As I help her to sit up, putting pillows behind her to support her back, she doesn't take her eyes off her son. I make a mental note to remember that saying '*don't worry*' to a woman whose new baby is crying is not actually going to make her feel any better.

"Shall we try him on this side?" I ask, picking Isaac up and moving him towards his mother.

Jessie shrugs, her gaze fixed on Isaac. "I don't mind," she says.

Of course, she doesn't. All she wants is for him to be happy and feeding rather than crying.

"Okay," I say. "So, if you hold him like this –" I place him in Jessie's arms in the best position. "– and you want to line him up here. His nose should be in line with your nipple there. That's right. When he opens his mouth move him in towards the –"

Isaac gapes widely on cue, and I support Jessie's hand on the back of his head, bringing him in to take a wide mouthful of breast.

Instead of latching and suckling he lets out a muffled sob and jerks back away from Jessie.

She flicks her eyes over towards me, and her expression is a mix of confusion and concern.

"Is he okay?" she asks.

"It can take a few tries sometimes," I tell her. I know that I need to remain calm and patient, not just for my own benefit, but so that my confidence passes onto Jessie. "Try to relax yourself back into the bed there. Drop your shoulders, that's it. It's all right."

If Jessie becomes anxious, Isaac probably will too.

"Let's try that again," I say, with a warm smile.

Jessie nods unconvincingly, and we run through the same set of moves.

Again, Isaac spits the breast from his mouth and pulls back from Jessie.

Again, we repeat the process.

Although I am trying to keep my thoughts together and not show any signs of frustration I am already starting to wonder if I am doing something wrong. Isaac appears completely fine apart from being hungry. He could have got himself over-anxious about the feed, maybe, possibly. I don't know.

"We can try taking off his sleepsuit, so his skin is against yours," I suggest. "Or we can change his position."

I'm thinking out loud, running through the options that I have tried before at other bedsides with other babies. I don't have a lot of experience to draw from, but I have enough, don't I?

The room is starting to feel particularly warm. No, it's not the room, it's me. I can feel the heat of my blood thudding rapidly through my body, the stress beginning to kick in. While Jessie is looking down at Isaac I take a quick deep breath.

"Don't worry," I say again, and I wonder if this time I'm talking to myself.

I unbutton the sleepsuit and Jessie pulls back the top of her pyjamas so that her infant can lie with his skin directly against hers. We lay him so that Jessie is comfortable, and Isaac is perfectly aligned for the feed, but he still doesn't latch when she moves him towards her.

"What other positions can we try?" she asks.

"I…I…" I stutter, and look her in the eye. "Perhaps I should go and find one of the other midwives and see if they can give us a hand," I say.

It's not so much that I think I can't do this, but I'm starting to believe that Isaac is getting more and more distressed because of me. Because I am failing. He is almost screaming, and Jessie's expression is becoming increasingly desperate. I don't know if I can help them. I need to find someone who can.

"Sometimes –" I start to explain and then stop myself. "Someone more experienced will be able to get him feeding and settled," I say. "I'm sure."

She nods, once, silently. I don't see any traces of annoyance or blame in her expression, but I still feel guilty. I still feel as though I have let her down.

"I'll only be a minute," I reassure her. "I'll grab one of the other midwives and come straight back."

"Okay," she says, running her hand softly over Isaac's head, trying to soothe him.

"I'm sorry." I say the words as I open the door and walk onto the corridor. I don't know what else to say.

My heart is in my mouth as the chaos of the ward hits me. Everything feels like it's moving too quickly around me, almost as though I'm at a train station at rush hour.

"Hey. Are you all right?"

I can't focus at first. My head is spinning. I steady myself with one hand against the wall, trying yet again to keep myself together.

"Hey. Violet?"

It's Beth.

Okay. Okay.

I take a breath.

"I'm fine," I lie.

I know she must be able to hear the sound of the crying baby inside the room behind us. I feel like I should apologise to her too. It's my fault that he is upset. He's making that noise because I failed him. I don't say that. I don't show how I feel. Instead I gesture towards the door, and give a weak smile.

"Feeding trouble," I explain. "Do you think you could give me a hand?"

Beth looks at me for a split second, hesitating before she gives her smiling response. "Sure. I can try," she says.

Something about the way that she paused makes my heart sink. Am I making a bad first impression by asking for help so soon? Is this something that I should be able to do without getting someone else involved?

"Great," I say. "Thanks. And sorry. I know you're probably busy down your end."

Beth shakes her head.

"Not at all. I was just about to work out where the kettle was and make us all some tea. Once we've got this baby feeding, you can show me."

"Sounds like a fair deal," I say. I feel sick, and I don't think I could face tea right now, but sitting down in the office for five minutes is exactly what I need.

Back with Jessie, I introduce Beth and step back to give the three of them space.

Beth unwraps the blanket and works with Jessie to position Isaac so that he is tucked beneath her arm, skin to skin, in what we refer to as the rugby hold. His head is supported by Jessie's hand, his weight by her arm and a pillow below it, and his eyes gaze directly up at his mother. With Beth's assistance, Jessie lines Isaac's nose up with her nipple, and they wait for exactly the right moment, when Isaac's mouth is wide open and in the perfect position to receive the breast. On the first attempt, as Jessie brings him towards her, he closes his jaw too soon, and clamps his lips firmly shut. She looks up at Beth with disappointment rather than frustration in her eyes.

"It's okay," Beth tells her. "Give him a few seconds and you can line him up again. He'll get there. You'll get there. I promise."

Her northern accent is soft and soothing, and Jessie nods silently, turning her gaze back to her son.

"Okay, now, yes, that's it…" Beth's hand is lightly guiding Jessie's, bringing the baby back in the right direction, showing his once-more-open mouth how to reach the breast.

The nipple points up towards his palate and with one swift movement his pink lips curl around a mouthful of breast, and he is there, perfectly positioned.

"You made that look easy," I say without thinking.

"She did, didn't she?" Beth smiles, although I'm sure we both know that my careless words were aimed at her. Of course, it's Jessie that needs to hear the encouragement and support, not the midwife.

"How does that feel?" Beth asks her.

Jessie nods cautiously, as if not wanting to move too much and risk displacing her baby.

"Fine, yes. Good."

"It doesn't hurt at all?" Beth asks.

"No, not at all."

"Great," Beth says. "It shouldn't hurt when you feed. When your milk starts to come in, in a couple of days, it might tingle for the first few seconds, but if it hurts, you need to reposition him okay?"

"Thanks," Jessie says. "I might need your help next time, if you don't mind."

"Of course not," Beth says.

Even though Isaac is feeding, and Jessie looks relaxed and calm now, my own feelings are mixed. Breastfeeding support is such a basic, fundamental part of my role, and I couldn't do it. Not only could I not do it, but now, next time my patient wants to feed her baby, she is going to want a different midwife to help her. She knows I failed. I know I failed. Beth knows I failed.

We leave the room together, Beth holding the door open for me as I pass through into the corridor. It's only when it closes behind her that she speaks.

"Hey," Beth says. "You okay?"

I nod, silently, and force myself to smile.

"He looks happy there," I say.

I know that I'm being ridiculous, really I do, but I can't help it. I feel disappointed in myself and stupidly jealous of Beth's effortless ability.

"Ready for that tea?" Beth asks.

"Sure," I say, trying to sound cheerful. "Thanks for that, Beth. I don't know what I was doing wrong."

"Probably nothing!" she says. "Don't worry about it. I'm sure I just got lucky, caught him at the right moment or whatever."

I shrug, as we walk along the corridor together.

"Sorry," I say. "It's my first day in the navy tunic today. I don't know if anyone told you."

We reach the kitchen as I finish the sentence, and she stops to look at me.

"Mine too," she says.

"It's not quite the same," I laugh.

Rather than joining in, she looks a little confused.

"Why's that?" she asks.

"I'm *new* new," I say. "First shift as a registered midwife. I did my training here though. Where were you before?"

"I trained in York," she says.

"And you worked there before you moved here?" I ask.

"What? No. I came straight here," she says, a look of recognition starting to dawn on her face. Oh gosh. I'm newly qualified too. I thought everyone knew."

I'm an idiot, but she looks so confident, and everything that I have seen her do has been so effortless and perfect.

"I could have started last week," she says, "but I wanted to wait for my PIN before I jumped in. I treated myself to a holiday. Student life was hard enough, right?"

I find myself nodding and smiling, although I also feel a cold smack of shock at the realisation that Beth is newly qualified, just as I am.

"Maybe I should have done that," I say. "Last week was so busy, and…"

"I'm glad it's not like that today. I was bricking it before I came here."

"But you look so calm!" I can't keep the surprise from my voice.

"I kind of feel calm now," she says. "Moving to a new town, starting work in a new hospital …there are a whole heap of challenges, I can tell you."

I gulp back my feelings and nod. She has so many more challenges than I do, and yet she's facing them head on, as though they were nothing. Her confidence makes me feel even more inadequate than ever before.

Is Becky going to judge me by Beth's capabilities? Am I falling behind already? What am I even doing here?

Instead of showing how I feel, and instead of speaking my mind I smile at my new colleague and help her with the tea. I can't break down now, in front of someone that barely knows me. I have to keep going. I have to show everyone that I can do this, that I can be as good as she is. First, I have to start believing that for myself, and right now, I can't. I really can't.

# Chapter Twelve

I can't use my phone when I'm on shift, so I leave it tucked away in my locker. On the bus home I check my messages.

**How was your first day as a real midwife? xx**

Zoe, of course. Because I'm still following Becky's shift pattern, my Monday mate date was postponed this week. I know I only saw her on Saturday, but not having our usual coffee, cake and chatter feels weird. Even though I know she's probably headed to bed already, I have to reply. My thumbs pause over the keypad while I wonder what to tell her. How was it?

I had three women and three babies to look after, and I couldn't handle even that.

I shake my head at my phone and put it into my pocket. I can't think about it now. I need to put those thoughts to one side, just for a little while.

I ride the bus home in a daze, trying to think about anything other than work.

When I get home, I throw my bag into the corner, settle onto the sofa, click my phone open again and type in my reply to Zoe.

**I survived xx**

I press send straight away, and then start tapping at the keys again.

**There's another new midwife and she's brilliant. xx**

It doesn't quite tell the whole story, but Zoe knows how to read between the lines.

**YOU'RE brilliant xx** comes the response.

I smile at the screen briefly, before snapping my expression back to a flat-faced frown. Reading those words from Zoe gives me a warm glow, but I know they aren't true. She says these things because she is my best friend and because we support each other. I know though that today I was far from brilliant.

**I missed Coffee Express xx**

I want to change the subject. There's no point weighing Zoe down with my boring shift and my even more boring anxiety. I want to think happy thoughts and enjoy the short amount of time I have before I have to get ready for bed and get the few hours of sleep I can before I have to get up and go back to the ward in the morning.

**Same. I had cake at home though xx**

She sends a gif of a bear eating a huge slice of cake, and this time I can't stop my smile.

Another text from her follows.

**I'll buy you an extra-large slice tomorrow xx**

I should probably stick to a regular sized piece, and to be honest I should probably try to cut down on the amount of cake I eat in general. I'm not exactly fat, but I must be at least a couple of sizes bigger than Beth. She's so trim and full of energy. I look like a bumbling chubby idiot next to her. How can she be newly qualified and still have everything completely under control? How can she walk onto a new unit where she has never worked before and fit in so effortlessly? I'm struggling to make the change from student to qualified midwife on a ward I trained on, with midwives that supported me as a student and support me still. What's her secret?

I send Zoe a gif in return, because I don't want to agree to the extra cake, but I know her intentions are only good. Scrolling through the options, I pick out a cute rabbit turning to the viewer and giving a cheeky thumbs up gesture. Sometimes pictures say far more than words, and sometimes I don't want to talk about what's really on my mind.

It's half-past ten and I'm exhausted. I treat myself to a low-fat hot chocolate and settle onto the sofa. Before I put my phone down onto the table I have the sense to set my alarm. Six-thirty am. If I went to bed and fell asleep straight away I'd just about get the eight hours of beauty sleep that the experts say we need. The experts have clearly never had to work shifts. I look at the numbers on the screen for a second and shake my head. This is my future. From now until the time that I hang up my gloves and retire I'll be working this pattern of earlies, lates and night shifts. I'll be limiting my social life, screwing with my sleep pattern, and probably giving up all hope of a normal routine and regular relationship. All this, for what? To call on other midwives for help because I can't even carry out the simplest of tasks.

If I can't even help a mother to breastfeed, what can I do?

Back on the unit, I'm at the same end of the ward, with the same allocation of women. That's the good thing about back-to-back shifts, at least there's continuity of care. For the women it means that they don't have to keep seeing different faces, and for both of us it means there's a chance to build up a relationship, even if most of them on the postnatal ward are short-lived now.

Aisling is reading a book when I arrive at her bedside. She could probably have gone home yesterday, she's so chilled and in control, I'm sure she'll be wanting to be discharged this morning.

"How are you feeling?" I ask, never assuming anything.

"Great," she says. "Little rabbit's asleep." She nods towards the cot, and I smile at the nickname she's already chosen for her baby.

"I can come back and check him over when he wakes up," I say. "No hurry."

There's no rush. I have three women to care for, and I can do this.

"I was hoping to go home for lunch," she says.

"That should be fine," I tell her. "I'll need to do your postnatal check. The doctor has already cleared the rabbit to leave the hutch." I feel stupid as soon as I say it, but Aisling just smiles.

"Great," she says again.

"You've been feeling okay?"

"Super," she says. "Everything is so easy."

She certainly looks comfortable and confident. I run through her postnatal check but as she's pulling her pyjama top back down over her abdomen I stop and stand up sharply.

There's a baby crying, but I don't know where the sound is coming from. It's not the usual sound that is so common on the ward, that recognisable newborn wail. This cry is different. My intuition triggers, and I know that I have to drop everything to go and find where the noise is coming from.

"I'm sorry," I say to Aisling. "I need to go and check on that baby." Not wanting to alarm her, I keep my voice calm and reassuring. "I'll be right back," I smile.

"No problem," she says, and goes back to reading her book as I leave.

The corridor is strangely free of people. I'm used to the bustle of staff, if not midwives then domestics, support workers and various doctors. There's no one in sight. It makes sense. If anyone else could hear the baby's cries I'm sure they would be looking for him too.

My eyes blink involuntarily as I realise that I know this is a male infant. Intuition again? Baby boys and baby girls sound very much the same when they're crying. I know this is a boy. I can almost picture him, and I try to focus in on my feelings as I listen to work out where he is.

The nursery seems like an obvious place to start. His cry is definitely coming from the middle of the corridor. Near the midwives' office, which I see is empty as I pop my head in on the way past. Pushing the nursery door open, I see that there's a cot pushed up against the far wall. The crying has paused, and I run over to the plastic cot to look inside. There's a pile of blankets inside, too many for a newborn, and my brain instinctively thinks that I need to take some off, uncover him, unwrap him, make sure he's not too hot. That's why he's crying, surely?

As I remove one layer of blankets after another, I hear the crying again, but it's not coming from this cot. All that's in here is a pile of knitted covers. No baby. Not here.

"Where are you?" I say out loud, even though the only response I expect is more crying.

I've got a strange feeling that something bad is happening, and I wonder whether I should go and find help. It could just be my anxiety kicking in, and I don't want to make an idiot of myself. I have to look first, and besides, there's no one around to help me anyway.

"Isaac?" I call. Of course, he can't answer. "Isaac?"

I pause in the hallway, outside the linen cupboard, and the crying is definitely louder here.

There's a small square window set into the door, and I stand on my tiptoes to look inside.

Sheets and towels are stacked on the shelves, but on the floor at the bottom there's a small blue blanket-wrapped bundle.

"What…" I look up and down the corridor, hoping to catch sight of someone, not quite knowing what to do first – call for help or grab the baby. I still can't see anyone. Pick him up then, make sure he's safe.

I push the door and the sound of his yelling is deafening. Surely someone else must have heard him, but no one has come for him. There's only me. I have to help him, but I don't know what to do.

Bending down next to him, I scoop him up into my arms and lift him from the floor. He's swaddled in the blanket, his arms and legs tucked neatly within the blue woollen knit. Despite his yells, his face is pink and shows no sign of distress. I can feel the relief course through me.

"Ssh," I say, stroking his head gently. "You're going to be fine now. It's okay."

He stares at me, open-mouthed, and his cries stop at the sound of my voice.

Despite the fact that he looks unharmed and appears well I know that I need to let someone know that he was left here, get a doctor to check him over…what else do I need to do?

He continues to look at me as I feel my anxiety build.

Who do I tell? Do I take him straight back to Jessie? Do I take him to the nursery and call the ward sister? Beth would know what to do. My legs have turned to stone, and I am frozen with no idea of what to do next.

The baby stares at me in silence, and I look back at him in inept panic.

I don't know how long I stand there before the quiet is pierced by the sound of a call bell going off. I know that I have to answer it, but I can't leave this baby here alone. There's nowhere to put him, and I can't carry him with me.

"Can someone get that?" I call out.

I should carry him out of here, but should I take him back to his mother, put him safely in his cot or in the nursery? I can't do either. For some reason I can't move. I'm stuck here, staring at this child, listening to the buzzer, trying to soothe him, but knowing that there's nothing I can do.

"Can someone help me?" I shout, but no sound comes out of my mouth.

I look down at the baby again, and his eyes fix upon mine.

Sometimes when a mother is cradling a baby in her arms, their eyes lock with such emotion that it's almost palpable to the observer. Right now, that's what is happening to me. I can feel the force of that gaze, the feelings…the…

My neck aches, my legs are stiff. I open one eye, and then the other, and reach out for my phone. It's not where I should be. I'm not where I should be. I'm on the sofa instead of being in my bed. Of course, there's no baby, there's no call bell sounding, there's just the sound of my alarm going off.

I let out a dull groan. The pain in my body and the realisation that it's time to start getting ready for work hit me in a double whammy. It all felt so real. My hopeless, helpless brain has let me down again.

Turning off my alarm, I sit on the edge of the sofa and let my face flop down into my hands. Late nights, early mornings, bad dreams. Is this really my future?

My heart thuds double time as I pull myself up and to my feet. When I look in the bathroom mirror I see a clammy, pale ghost of myself looking back at me. The helpless, useless feeling that I had in my dream is still there, even though I'm awake now.

"Get a grip," I tell myself.

I want to listen. I have to listen. I have half an hour to pull myself together, get ready for work and leave to face another shift. It's the last thing I feel like doing.

Splashing cold water over my cold, moist face I think the words again. "Get a grip."

The problem is that I don't know what to grip onto. I don't know how to snap out of this and stop feeling this…whatever it is. Anxiety, sure, but this feels like more than that. It feels like fear. Fear of failure. Fear of not being good enough. Fear of everyone else being better than I am. Fear of letting people down.

# Chapter Thirteen

Nine hours later I walk into Coffee Express, head straight for the table where Zoe is sitting and flop towards her into a sloppy embrace.

"That bad?" she asks, pulling back from me to look at my expression.

Nodding, I nuzzle back into her. I need this hug too much to let go just yet.

"Hey," she says. "Hey, it's okay."

I wasn't going to be like this. I told myself repeatedly on the way home from work, while I was stumbling around my flat getting ready to come here, while I was walking down to Coffee Express, over and over I told myself that I was going to keep my feelings hidden. Not that I don't think I can talk to Zoe, of course I know I can, but I wanted this evening to be a distraction from how I am feeling. I want to hear about Zoe and Luke, talk about the wedding, think happy thoughts. Now there's no hope of that. Instead of showing up with a smile on my face I've crashed in with tears in my eyes.

"Vi. Ssh." Zoe strokes my hair and whispers into my ear. "Come on, sit down. Let me get your latte and we can talk about it."

I thought I would shake my head and refuse the offer, but instead I nod and draw back to allow her to break from our clumsy cuddle.

Zoe puts her hand gently onto my arm before walking to the counter to pick up my usual order, and I dab at my stupid tears as I watch her. She barely takes her eyes off me, even when she's talking to the barista. That look on her face – the compassionate, concerned expression – every time I see it, I'm floored by the mixed emotions it stirs in me. On one hand I'm overwhelmed by how much my best friend cares about me, and on the other I feel guilty and completely useless for being in such a ridiculously dependent state. Every time, because this is not the first time that I've come to her like this, and I know that it probably will not be the last.

The feelings I am having, the stress of adapting to my new job, the anxiety that comes with the new, none of them are going to be cured by coffee and cake, but perhaps talking to Zoe, really, honestly talking to her, perhaps that's a good place to start.

Zoe slides a small plate bearing a large slab of Bakewell slice towards me and sets my latte down beside it.

"Have you even eaten today?" she asks as she settles back into the seat beside me.

"Yeah," I say. "The ward wasn't even busy." Admitting that to her almost brings another onslaught of tears.

"What's happened then, Vi? What's going on?"

I can't answer. I haven't got hold of the right words yet, so I stick my fork into the end of the Bakewell and take a chunk of the almondy cake into my mouth.

"Is it one of the midwives? Is someone being mean to you?"

Her tone sounds so intense, as though if I said that yes, this was the problem, she would be straight down at the unit to confront whoever it was that had upset me.

I shake my head, and swallow down the sweet mouthful.

"It's me," I say. "It's all just me."

Zoe is leaning in towards me but even though I know that there's no one near enough to hear our hushed conversation I still feel self-conscious. I flash a look around us.

"Did you want to go back to mine to talk about it?" she asks, reading my actions rather than reading my mind.

"No," I say without hesitation. "I don't want to bring all of my negativity to your home."

"Oh Vi. I hate seeing you like this."

"I hate feeling like this. I can't even put my finger on anything specific that's happened to make me such a wobbling wreck."

"You're not –" She begins to speak, but I raise my fork-wielding hand like a stop sign.

"I am," I say. "I'm useless. Don't say I'm not. Right now, I am completely useless. It's not even been two weeks yet and already I'm dreading going into work. And last night I hardly slept..." I let my sentence trail off.

"Because of work stress?"

I sigh and lean back.

"I fell asleep on the sofa and had a bad dream," I tell her. "About work."

She purses her mouth into a tight frown and strokes my arm gently. "Want to talk about it?"

"It was stupid. I dreamt that I was on the ward, and I could hear this baby crying and he was in the cupboard and..." I stop again. "I don't suppose any of it makes sense to you. It was more about how I was feeling, how the dream made me feel. I didn't know what to do. I was second guessing myself, panicking, and, well, pretty much doing nothing." I force myself to look Zoe in the eye. "That's how I feel at work when I'm not dreaming. It's as though I can't do anything right, or I want to ask someone for a second opinion for every decision I make. I'm...I suppose I'm not adjusting very well."

"It's all so new, Vi," Zoe says, her voice as calming and reassuring as ever. "Being a student and getting out there into the real world of work isn't an easy step."

"Beth thinks it is," I say, and immediately feel ridiculous.

"Beth?"

"The new midwife. The other new midwife."

The link between the name and the messages I sent her last night seems to fall into place for Zoe.

"Right," she says. "I get it now."

There's a moment of silence between us, and then Zoe speaks again.

"Do you not like her?"

I shrug, wafting my hands so hard that I almost knock the rest of my cake to the floor.

"She's wonderful," I sigh. "Honestly, she is so good. She's helpful and cheerful and all the other good –ful words. Beautiful." I roll my eyes with a childish flourish of annoyance and try to force a smile.

"Well, she sounds…" Zoe looks at me before she finishes her sentence. "She sounds very much like you."

Again, I shake my head hard, refuting Zoe's claim.

"She's nothing like me. She's the opposite of me. And the thing is everyone else can probably see that, you know. It's not just that I am new and a little bit rubbish because I'm just starting out. She is starting out too, in a new ward, a new hospital, and she breezes through it like she's some kind of Super Midwife."

"Oh love. You can't go comparing yourself to other people like that. Maybe she spends all her free time reading textbooks and polishing her halo." Zoe bites her lip. "No," she says. "If you say she's lovely, she probably *is* lovely. We're not going to sit here saying bad things about her."

"Reading textbooks isn't such a bad thing," I smile. Neither me nor Zoe are the type to bitch and snipe about other people though, not even someone who makes me feel inadequate by just existing. "It's my issue, not hers. You're right."

"Right," she says, brightening, and then snapping her expression back to her concerned gaze. "I mean, it's your issue and in a way that makes it something that you can deal with, right. The way you *feel* is your issue."

I let myself scoop a little more of the cake into my mouth while I think it over.

"I should probably talk to Becky again," I sigh. "I just…I wanted to be able to get over the first few weeks, get over myself, get into the swing of things. I wanted to do this without getting help."

"You always want to struggle on, Vi," Zoe says. "You don't want counselling, you don't want meds, you don't want to talk about how you feel."

"Because I feel stupid." I almost snap the words, but I don't let my reflex reaction get the better of me. "I'm sorry. Feeling like this, feeling so stupid makes me get so defensive, you know how it is."

"I do," she says. "But there are people that want to help you. I'm always here, you know that, but from what you've told me before it sounds like you can talk to Becky."

"She's been through it too, you know. Anxiety. Depression. Not that I'm depressed, I'm not, I'm just stressed and stupid, stupid, stupid."

"Stop it," Zoe commands. "You're a qualified midwife. You got through your course. You passed your exams, you aced your assignments and you beat your own self-doubt to get to where you are now. There's nothing stupid about you, so stop it."

I'm aware of a couple at the next table lowering their voices, softening their conversation, no doubt so that they can listen in to our heated debate. I don't want to look around the room because I'm already almost certain that everyone will be staring at us. Zoe wasn't loud, but her words feel powerful enough to attract attention.

I let my fork clatter onto the empty plate, and I push my seat out from the table, just a little, just enough to give me some breathing space.

"I'm so sorry," I say. "Everything is always about me, isn't it? Why can't we be like regular people, getting excited about your wedding plans, chatting about what we've been watching on television, whatever it is that normal people do?"

"We're just us," she says without batting an eyelid. "We're Zoe and Violet. We talk about whatever we need to talk about, and right now, we need to talk about how you can start enjoying your dream job…"

"…instead of feeling like it's a nightmare." Despite the negative words, we smile at each other, and she raises the dregs of her mocha to clink coffee cups with me.

"Thanks, Zo. I think I needed to offload, you know."

"And cake always helps, right?"

The mood has lightened, but the look of concern still shines through Zoe's calm countenance.

"You will talk to Becky again, won't you?" she asks quietly.

"I will," I say, but the words are a reflex response rather than a firm commitment.

"If you absolutely promise that you will make time to do when you're next on shift I'll show you something…"

"Hmm?" My eyebrows instinctively bounce upwards in curious surprise. "What? What are you holding out on me?"

She beams. "Promise first?"

"Okay, okay," I say.

"And mean it."

I sigh and let my genuine smile shine through. "I will," I tell her. "I want to enjoy being on the unit. I do." I take a breath, look at my best friend and ask, "I will be okay, won't I?"

She leans in towards me again, wrapping her arms around me, and squeezing me tightly against her.

"You will," she breathes into my hair. "You will."

I let myself relax into her embrace, taking in the scent of her soft floral perfume.

"Okay," I say eventually. "No more stalling. What have you got to show me?"

Zoe wiggles excitedly, and reaches down into her bag.

All this time the surprise has been there, and she has carried it secretly while she listened to me moan about my problems. Not once did she try to turn the attention to herself. Not once did she ask for anything from me. Now though, I can see how much this means to her.

"Invitations!" she squeaks, wiping away invisible crumbs and laying a heavy brown envelope onto the table.

"Yes!" I squeal in return.

I'm muddling through, getting by on a day-to-day basis and Zoe is absolutely bossing it. In three months, she will be married to a gorgeous, adorable man, and I will probably still be waking up alone on the sofa.

"Show me!" I prompt, and she does.

# Chapter Fourteen

I'm not sure which I am hoping for most: that it's a quiet day on the ward so I can talk to Becky, or that Beth isn't on shift with me today. It sounds awful, and I don't mean it with any malice towards her, but the more time I spend with her the worse I feel about myself and my own skills.

It doesn't help that she and I are the only newly qualified midwives in the unit. There was only one other student from my year group based at St. Jude's with me, my course mate Sophie. She upped and moved on to be with her girlfriend and live a city life in London. Her and our other course colleague, Simon both moved down to the capital city, away from the seaside backwater of Cranbourne. It never crossed my mind to leave this area. I was born in Portland, less than an hour away. I grew up in that nearby town, and my mum still lives there. Of course, Zoe is here, but I also thought that staying in the unit that I trained in would make the transition to being a qualified member of staff easier.

Sophie. I wonder what she's doing now. I was bad enough at keeping in touch with her and my other class colleagues when I was studying, never mind now we are separated by miles. Our phones may be able to connect us with anyone, anywhere, at any time, but mine can't cure my social anxiety and ineptitude.

"Daydreaming?" Becky grins at me as she walks into the midwives' office. There's a full ten minutes until the start of our late shift, but I've already made the tea and settled into one of the more comfortable seats to wait for handover.

"A little bit," I smile back. "Wondering how Sophie is getting on."

"You're not in touch with her?" She sounds more surprised than I might have expected. Becky knows me, after all.

I shrug. "I should try harder. I've been busy. I've been…" I shake my head. "I've been pretty lazy about keeping in touch."

"Happens to us all," Becky says, with a hint of sadness to her voice. "I only keep in contact with the midwives I trained with that still work here. You get in that routine of work, sleep, work, recover."

*Tell me about it.* I think the words, but don't say them.

"How's it going now anyway?" Becky asks, wrinkling her face as though trying to analyse me without waiting for an answer.

"Ugh," I say, without trying to cover my feelings. "I was going to ask if we could have a chat, actually. If it's not too much –"

"It's not too much anything. That's what I'm here for. That's why you have a preceptorship mentor." She turns her eyes to the heavy book on the desk that lists the women who are currently occupying each of the beds or rooms on the ward. The ward appears quiet, and the sparsely populated list seems to confirm it. "Unless we have a mad rush we should be fine." She touches her hand against the wooden desk.

"Touch wood," we both say at the same time.

It's a silly superstition, but despite being scientifically minded, we do seem to stick to some of those. Never talk about the ward being *quiet*; it's bound to lead to the kind of influx that Becky just mentioned.

It takes me next to no time to do my rounds and make sure the women and babies under my care are comfortable and have everything they need. There are no beds to be made, no errands to run, and the teapot in the office has already been refilled. For every busy day when we work for hours without breaks, there are days like this. Well, perhaps not for *every* busy day, but there is certainly a kind of balance over the months.

There's enough time for me to sit at the heavy wooden desk and write in my ladies' notes before Becky returns and takes the seat beside me.

"You okay?" she asks, nodding towards the paperwork.

"Yep," I reply. "Everyone is happy."

"Including you?"

I deflect by turning to the last postnatal record and tidying it neatly into its folder.

"We can go and have that chat now, if you're ready." Becky says.

However much I want to get everything out of my system, I can't shake the feeling that my concerns aren't worth distracting Becky with. I don't want to waste her time. I don't want to waste my time. We could be helping to make beds, giving the other midwives a hand or –

"Don't worry about everyone else," Becky says, as if reading my mind. "You are important too. This is all part of your preceptorship. We're supposed to be having regular chats to go through anything that you need to talk about."

Reluctantly I face her again and reply. "Thanks, Becky."

"Come on, let's grab a brew and go back to the seminar room."

I follow her down the corridor, to the kitchen and then onwards to our meeting place.

The two of us sit, and she asks me a question that I should have prepared myself better to answer.

"How are things?"

There's so much to say that I don't know where to start.

The chairs are comfortable in here, so comfortable that the night staff sometimes use them for naps during their breaks. The fabric on the arm of my seat is starting to fray, and there's a loose strand within reach of my fingers that I can't help but nervously pick at.

Becky patiently sips her tea, watching me.

I expect her to fill the silence, to ask another question, to say something, anything, but she doesn't. Instead she drinks her tea and waits.

My mind is whirring through all the different responses that I could offer. Things are no better. Things are worse. I can't do this. I don't know what I'm doing. I feel like a failure. I can't do what Beth can do. I can't do what anyone else can do.

"I don't know," I say, eventually. "I'm still finding it really difficult."

Becky nods. "Tell me more about how you're feeling."

"I suppose I…well, it's a confidence issue. At least I think it is. Confidence, anxiety, same thing in a lot of ways. I'm not good enough. I don't deserve to be here."

Becky points at my name badge. The badge that was taped over until I received my PIN, that now reads "Registered Midwife Violet Cobham".

"What does it say?" she asks me.

I read my title and name out loud.

"Registered Midwife Violet Cobham."

"That's you, isn't it? I'm not going to have to call security to come and remove an imposter, am I?"

I try to smile, but I can't.

"It's me, but…"

"But nothing. Violet Cobham you deserve to be here because you worked hard to train and qualify as a midwife. You studied, you put in your hours on the wards, and you passed. That badge says so."

They're just words on plastic. What do they mean if I don't believe in them? If I don't believe in myself? I look at the photo embedded next to my name and title. I look so happy, so excited. It was taken three weeks ago, after I qualified, before I started work. How can things have changed so much in such a short time?

"I can't make you believe me, Violet. You need to find that within yourself. I know probably better than anyone that telling you that you're great isn't going to convince you. You are. You are great. You have to feel it in here though."

She pats her soft, safe hand against her chest, over her heart.

"You have to learn to trust yourself, just like the women that you care for trust you. And they do."

I take a deep breath, and let it out slowly.

"And I do. I trust you. I signed off your antenatal placements. I would never have done that if I didn't believe in you. I wanted to be your preceptorship mentor; I volunteered to support you because I believe in you."

"Thanks, Becky," I say. "That means a lot."

A warm glow is beginning to blossom within me, and it's not from the tea I am nervously sipping as my mentor speaks.

"We've all been there, and we have all felt the feelings that you're feeling," she says. "Some to a lesser degree, but I can assure you that the transition is difficult for everyone."

She pauses and takes another drink, then sets her cup down on the table.

"Can you ride a bike?" she asks.

"What? Er, yes," I reply, taken off guard.

"I was about eight years old when my gran taught me how. My mum worked until six o'clock, and I stayed with my gran between the end of school and when my mum came to collect me. There was this park near where Granny lived, with a wide-open field. Flat, short grass, perfect for cycling lessons. I started out with stabilisers, when I was first learning, but as I got better, as I learned to balance she would hold on to me, gently, ever so gently, giving me enough support to stay upright and keep moving forward. I would pedal along, slowly enough for her to keep up with me, feeling the fresh air on my face and the smooth, soft ground beneath the wheels. I always knew that she was there, holding on to me, keeping me steady."

Becky wipes at her eye with her forefinger and sniffs in a short sharp breath, pausing.

"I miss her," she says. "So much." She breathes and continues. "One day, we set off just as we had every other day. I pushed my feet against the pedals, gripped the handlebars and trundled across that field…but I went faster, it felt different, somehow. 'Don't let go!' I said. 'Don't let go!' But of course, she already had. I was doing it on my own. My little legs were pumping, my knuckles were white, and my heart was going like the clappers. But I was doing it on my own. I couldn't look over my shoulder to see her, I was too focused on the field ahead of me, moving in the right direction, keeping the momentum going, but I knew she would be smiling. I knew she would be proud."

Becky's voice breaks on the last sentence and she raises her hand to cover her face.

I extend my arm and gently touch hers.

"She must have meant a lot to you," I say. "I'm sorry."

She dabs her eyes again and nods. "Thanks, Violet. When she caught up with me, she gave me the biggest hug. The look on her face, that pride, I'll never forget it. She knew exactly what to do to support me. I'm here for you, Violet. I'm right behind you. Your training was your stabilisers, and now I am here, my hand on your back. You can feel me next to you, but you are doing everything yourself. One day, one day soon, you will move forwards and you won't even notice that I'm not holding on to you anymore."

I don't know how to respond. Her words have touched me so deeply that I'm almost on the edge of tears too.

"I know it's true because those feelings I had with my gran, they are so similar to what I felt when I qualified as a midwife. I was as anxious as you are."

My hand is still on her arm, and I pat it softly in acknowledgement. "I know," I say. "I know you've been through this too."

"Of course, I was going through it with the other girls I trained with. Jade, Abigail, Megan. We were all in it together. At any given moment at least one of us would be either in tears in the sluice room or handing a cup of tea and box of tissues to one of the others. Midwifery is not an easy job, and if you ever thought that it was going to be you're dafter than I thought you were."

I manage a small smile.

"I know you didn't," she says. "And I know about all the other stuff you have going on. It's tough trying to manage your own feelings, caring for women going through these amazing emotional highs and lows, getting your head around the immense responsibility of being responsible for two lives at every bedside." She pauses and corrects herself. "Sometimes more. Sometimes less."

I nod. "I know. I do. I didn't take this on lightly. I know I'm my own worst enemy. I can never let myself feel good about anything. I can't let myself relax and enjoy what I have achieved, and what I am doing, because I worry all the time that I am doing something wrong. With Beth around it's a constant reminder that I could be doing things better. It's totally possible, because she is doing it. Everything that I am struggling with, she is breezing through."

Becky looks at me as I finish speaking, and I break eye contact.

"You know, I want to tell you that it's ridiculous to think like that. Part of me thinks that I should give you a figurative shake and get you to stop being so flipping negative." She leans towards me conspiratorially. "But I've felt those feelings that you're feeling. I've fought those battles against myself that you are fighting now. I was lucky, in a way, that my anxiety started later on. I was already a qualified midwife, settled in my job, confident in my skills, when my relationship broke down and my life started to fall to pieces. That's what started it for me. That's when my anxiety crept in, bedded down and decided it was staying."

"It didn't stay though," I say. "I mean, you're okay now."

"I'm mostly fine. Sure," she says. "But there's enough of it left in me for me to recognise what you're going through, and I have felt enough of it to have a good idea of how you are feeling."

I let out a slow, long sigh.

"What I can tell you though is that comparing yourself to Beth is pointless. She's a skilled midwife, sure. She's good at what she does, and the women have all taken to her. I like her, and as far as I know the rest of the team do too. But that's what we're like, isn't it? Welcoming. We're a team. We might get our own allocations of women and babies to look after, and we might look after our own caseloads, but at the end of the day we are a team. If any of us need any help, if there are any jobs that need to be done, we work together, we stick together. It's hard to be a midwife without being a feminist."

My eyes meet hers again, and I feel some of the tension in my body begin to subside.

"It is," I agree. "And I love the community. It's so great that we can sit here like this and talk. I feel like you understand me. Not just because you've been through something similar; I think you would understand me if you had never had an anxious thought in your life."

"Doesn't everyone feel like that sometimes though?" she smiles.

I nod and continue. "What I mean is…I've never given birth. I haven't experienced first-hand what the women I care for have been through, but I can empathise. I can be there for them and support them regardless of that fact."

"You remember that," Becky says. "Because there will be those who question that. Not because they doubt your training or your empathy, but because they wonder how you can care for them after their Caesareans when you have never had one yourself, or…" Again, she pauses, as if wondering whether to continue. "Whether you can support someone through a still birth when you have never felt that loss."

We take a few silent seconds to reflect on Becky's words.

"Being a midwife is tough," she says again. "Being a woman is tough. Being a mother is tough. But Violet. You can do this. You *are* doing this."

I have repeated these words to myself so many times, and perhaps I have come close to believing them in the past. Now, coming from Becky's mouth, they sound clear and true.

"Do you still doubt yourself sometimes?" I ask, timid as a mouse.

Her answer is a slow, steady nod.

"Don't expect that you will ever know everything. You have to give yourself a break. Give yourself permission to fail, to be flawed, to need support."

I reach out towards her, and she extends a hand in return. The two of us sit beside each other in the sunlit seminar room, separated from the ward by only a thin, cheap door, but we could be a thousand miles away. The stress and the pressure fall from me, as though I am shedding my skin, or emerging from a chrysalis. My whole life has led me to the moment that I am experiencing right now. I carry the pain and the emotional scars of my pre-teen and early teenage years, an emotionally abusive father and my struggles with the anxiety and self-doubt that stemmed from how he made me feel. I bear the courage and strength that I drew from those experiences. I made the decision to become a midwife as I was going through the worst days of my life. It wasn't only to help and support other women, the women journeying through pregnancy, birth, and life with their new families, but it was a move to help and support my own mental wellbeing. Midwifery was truly a vocation for me. I was called by something that I didn't realise was calling me at the time - but I know that I was called. There was never any other path that I wanted to walk.

"This is all I ever wanted," I tell Becky.

"Me too," she says. "And Violet, you are going to be an amazingly wonderful midwife who enjoys her days on the unit and looks forward to being back on the ward. You don't need your stabilisers anymore, and even when you don't need my hand on your back to support you, you'll know that I am always here. We are all here."

We sit together in the quiet, calm seminar room for a little longer. There's a charge in the air that I can't put into words. Something like the change in atmosphere that comes with the first sunny days of spring. The first signs of sunshine after the grey of winter, the warmth and knowing that when you set out for your walk, you're not going to need your hat and scarf anymore. Better days are coming. Of course, it's autumn now, and the late afternoon light won't last much longer. By the time I get to the end of my shift, it will be dark and cold, but this conversation with Becky is going to help me to see the sunny days ahead, and to focus on that warmth that I know I can feel.

I'm not sure whether it was the story that Becky told me about her cycling lessons or whether something inside me started to click, but the next few shifts are a lot less stressful and much more enjoyable.

When Beth sits down beside me at the start of our next late shift, I smile and there's no trace of the searing tension that has troubled me every time I've seen her up until now. Instead, I am calm, relaxed, and completely unfazed by her presence.

One of the women I looked after yesterday is still on the ward, and I'll be caring for her again today.

Being able to give continuity of care, seeing the same women from shift to shift can be just as rewarding for midwives as it can for the women themselves. We spent three hours yesterday talking about her pregnancy, her delivery, and her hopes for the future. We were building a relationship. The thought of spending more time with her, and the other women that I will be caring for today, makes me look forward to getting out of the office after handover and straight out onto the ward.

Time. Is that all this is about? Is that what really makes the difference? It's not everything, it's not the whole story, but it's such an important element of caring for someone.

"How's it going?" Beth asks, as handover finishes.

"I'm okay," I say. "It's going to be a good shift, eh?"

She looks down at the list of names that she has written on her handover sheet and nods.

"Unless those empty beds fill up," she says.

I give her a little smile and head down the corridor towards my end of the unit, carrying that smile with me all the way.

# Chapter Fifteen

My days off are Friday and Saturday, and I'm almost sad to be spending the time at home rather than at work. At least I would be if I didn't have dinner plans with Zoe and Luke. I make the most of my day at home, by reading some of the book I have been trying to get through for the past month. Even though I live alone, and should have all the time in the world I've found that by the time I get home I rarely have the motivation to click open my Kindle, let alone read. I do my washing, watch TV and finish three whole chapters, so by the time evening comes I'm nigh on exhausted by my hectic day. Nothing is going to stop me from getting up, getting dressed and going to Zoe and Luke's though. I drag myself to the bathroom, try to make myself look vaguely presentable, and head out into the cold autumnal night.

Luke's in the kitchen, which gives Zoe and I an opportunity to chat alone. Knowing the two of them they planned it this way, so that Zoe and I can gossip and natter before dinner and we can chill for the rest of the evening. Luke is my friend too, sure, but I don't think he needs to hear about my stresses and self-doubts. He's been there for me, and I'm grateful for that, but there are things that I only want to talk to my best friend about. Being the cool guy he is, Luke understands that.

Zoe hands me a glass of cola and flops on the sofa next to me.

“Busy day?” I ask her.

“Too many early mornings and not enough weekends,” she smiles. “Whoever decided there should be five workdays and only two weekend days was an idiot.”

“They’re all the same to me,” I smile back. “I’ve already pretty much forgotten what day it is. I know when I’m at work and when I’m not. The only reason I really know when it’s weekend is that you aren’t at work.”

“It’s a good job you know me then,” she says.

“Isn’t it?” We both grin at each other again, and she takes a large swig of her prosecco.

“I think I earned that. You sure you won’t have one?”

“Nah,” I say. “I’m trying to keep my head clear.”

“Anxiety?” she asks, her concerned look returning. “I thought things were starting to feel better?”

I shrug. “They are,” I say. “I don’t want to encourage them to get any worse. The more I can do to keep it away, the better.”

“Can’t argue with that. How have the last few days been?”

I run through the highlights without giving any of the details that might break any client confidentialities. She knows as well as I do that there are things we can't tell each other, so I sketch the outlines and she doesn't probe deeper.

"You sound so much more relaxed." Her smile shines through in her voice. It's only now that I realise how worried she has been about me, because the contrast is clear. "I'm so pleased, Vi." Then she gives me a worried look. "Do you think this is it now? Are you over the hump?"

"I don't know," I reply honestly. "I can't say for sure, but I feel so much better. I just need to keep pedalling onwards," I say with a smile. I don't explain the reference, but I don't have to. It works just as well as a figure of speech. "How's your week been?"

"I had my first visit from an anxious parent," she tells me. "Not *anxious* anxious," she clarifies, "Not proper anxiety, sorry. I mean, you know, she was worried about her daughter. Thought she may be going through some issues with one of her friends."

I nod. "Must be tough," I say. "Did you sort it out?"

"I hope so. It's difficult being a kid these days. It's only a few years since we left school, isn't it? But things seem so much more complicated for them now. It's all mobile phones and social media and constant pressure to keep up and fit in." She shakes her head with a frown. "We had it easy."

I complain so much about my own situation, and focus on the negative so often that I forget sometimes just how lucky I do have it.

"We did," I say. "We do."

As if to emphasise the point, Luke calls out from the kitchen.

"Dinner is served, ladies. Come on through."

After we have cleared the table and stacked the plates into the dishwasher the three of us settle back into the living room. In a way nothing has changed between us since they moved into this house and I moved to my flat. When the three of us are sitting together like this we could just as easily be hanging out in our old student residence, Tangiers Court. Zoe and Luke are snuggled on one sofa and I'm stretched out on the other. There's more room here, and the TV is bigger, but we still watch the same trashy programmes, and we still make the same old jokes.

"Have you shown Violet those pictures yet?" Luke says to Zoe, making my ears almost literally prick up in curiosity.

"Pictures?" She looks confused for a split second and then grins. "Oh, those pictures."

"The really amazingly sexy ones," he smiles.

"What's all this?" I'm curious, yes, but I'm starting to wonder whether I should really be involved in whatever it is he's goading her to show me.

"Pure porn," Zoe says, with a peel of laughter. "Your face, Vi. Priceless. It's nothing like that. Look."

She throws herself across from her seat next to Luke onto the sofa beside me, clicking open her phone and scrolling through her photo album.

"Are you sure about this?" I ask, my mind still heavy with doubt despite the couple's giggling.

"Food porn," she says, thrusting her phone into my hand.

The picture that she's flashing at me is a huge cake, a slice cut to show a rainbow-layered centre within the exterior plain white iced casing.

"What do you think?" she looks at me, more serious now, waiting for my opinion.

"Prim and proper on the outside and completely wild on the inside." It's my turn to laugh now. "Sums you two up perfectly," I say. "This is it then? The wedding cake?"

"One hundred per cent," Zoe says, scrolling on to the next photo, which shows a slab of the cake on a plate. "Doesn't it look amazing?"

"Have you tried it?" I ask. Even though we finished our lovely meal less than an hour ago I can almost taste the soft sweetness of cake on my lips, looking at the photos on Zoe's phone.

She nods rapidly, and looks over to Luke, who gives her another wide smile.

"I tried to convince him that it's bad luck for the groom to see the wedding cake before the ceremony, but he wasn't having any of it," she says.

"Zoe wanted to eat it all by herself, of course," he tells me. "She'll say anything, this one."

I can just imagine the pair of them filling the bakery with their playful banter. Part of me is so happy that my best friend has something so wonderful – someone so wonderful – in her life, and part of me wishes that I had been there too. So many changes. Once, all of the milestones in our lives were shared just between the two of us, and now she is starting out with Luke, sharing a life with him. So many changes.

"You're going to love it." Zoe puts her arm around me and gives me a little squeeze, as though reading my thoughts. "We've got the dresses, the cake, and…"

"We finally found our venue," Luke chimes in.

"Alright!" Zoe turns to him. "I can tell her!"

"I know. I'm excited too though," he smiles. "I'll go and make some tea. You fill her in on the details."

Luke busies himself in the kitchen as Zoe and I scroll through the photos on her phone of the amazing wedding venue that they have landed. It's not quite The Orangery, but at short notice they seem to have landed the perfect location for them.

If we still lived together, I'm sure that all we would do would be to talk about the upcoming wedding. Moving to a new house, starting our jobs, and living apart seems to have made us take a figurative step back as well as putting literal distance between us. In a way, it's probably good for Zoe and Luke that we have this space. They need time alone as a couple, and they should be able to plan their wedding without having me around chirping in all the time. Zoe would never see it that way, and I'm sure Luke wouldn't either, but I know in my heart that things are changing - and things need to change.

Whether Zoe is Miss Colebrook or Mrs Buxton she will always be my best friend.

# Chapter Sixteen

The following Monday is the first that I am actually on an early shift, and I can finally meet up with Zoe on our regular day. I'm still following Becky's rota for the most part, but now I'm also going to be having a few shifts without her. This time last week, the thought would have filled me with dread, but now I see it as an opportunity to test myself, to see whether I am truly starting to pedal without stabilisers.

The day starts like every other day. I greet the ladies, check that they and their babies are all okay, and start the daily rounds. Everything feels more natural today, like I've aligned with the rhythm of the ward. I feel like I am stepping in time with the beat of the duties I need to carry out. Something has clicked, and I know it must have something to do with that sense of spring that I was feeling. It has everything to do with talking to Becky, and focusing ahead, moving forward.

I've given the meds to the ladies at my end of the ward, and I'm walking back up the corridor to the midwives' office when I hear a loud clatter from the storeroom. Pushing the door open, I expect to see that a drip stand has fallen over, or that someone has stacked the sterile packs too high again. I have time to sort this out. It's a good feeling.

The good feeling is ripped away as I look into the room.

Beth is leaning against a cupboard, her bum against its door, scanning the shelf in front of her. She doesn't seem able to find whatever is it she is looking for. At her feet is a small pile of bright blue plastic kidney dishes, to which she is paying no attention.

"Are you…okay?" I ask, tentatively.

The look on her face as she turns to me is flustered and ruddy.

"I can't find anything today. I came to look for a cover for the BiliBed, you know, those towelling things we out over the…well, of course you know. Sam told me they were in here on the middle shelf, but I can't see them anywhere." She turns back to the shelf and her eyes flick backwards and forwards.

I can't help but look at the pile of dishes again.

"I heard a clatter," I say, less than helpfully. "Did you, I mean, did these fall from somewhere? Or...?"

I don't know what to say, really. She's completely disinterested in the mess on the floor, but from the way she is standing, looking blankly at the shelves without actually sifting through the stacked linen in search of the cover I'm not sure she's all that interested in finding what she says she is looking for. I'm completely bamboozled by this situation. Maybe it would help if I walked out, walked in again and started from the beginning.

I don't.

Instead I squat and start to collect the dishes. There are five of them in total, all well-used, scratched and past their best. They would originally have come from a delivery pack, or some other sterilised set, but now we use them for keeping our kit together when we need to take blood or give an injection. It's easier to carry everything in one of these bowls than to take all the individual items: needles, syringes, antiseptic wipes, cotton wool balls and micropore tape.

Beth doesn't help, but she doesn't try to stop me either. In fact, she says nothing, and appears to be in some kind of dazed stupor, her eyes moving over the blankets, sheets, and BabyGros that are neatly stacked on the open shelves. After I have put the dishes into the sink, ready to give them the once over before returning them to use, I stop.

"Are you sure you're okay?"

"Mmm, yes. Fine. Thanks."

She doesn't look at me, but she speaks again.

"I don't want to go back out there."

At first, I think I've misheard her, and I scrunch my eyes, trying to make sense of the words.

"You...what?"

"I don't want to go back out there," she says again. The same words in the same tone, so I can have no doubt.

This time, I reply. “Has something happened?” I ask.

She leans further against the cupboard, arching her back and letting her head flop, her gaze fixing on the white-painted ceiling.

“I messed up, and I can’t face trying again. The parents hate me. I just can’t.”

Again, it’s a lot to take in, and I try to dissect the meaning without losing her confidence.

There’s one thing I know for certain.

“Nobody hates you,” I say. “Why would you think that? What did you do?”

A chill shudders through me, but I shake it off. I can’t believe that Beth would do anything bad, or anything wrong. At least not intentionally, definitely not intentionally.

“Urgh,” she grunts.

I wait as she shakes her head, runs her fingers through her short blonde hair and brings her palms to rest over her face.

“I’m an idiot,” she says.

The words that I have spoken so many times are now coming out of someone else’s lips. I’m not used to being the one that listens to them rather than the one speaking them. I say what everyone always says to me, because what they say – and what I say now – is the truth.

“You’re not an idiot. Not at all.”

It's a strange feeling, being the one to reassure another person, rather than being the one who is worrying. I'm not used to playing this role with my peers.

"I'm sorry," she says. "You're probably busy. You don't have time for this. I'll go and talk to Sister. I should have done that in the first place instead of hiding in here."

"I have time," I tell her. "If I can help. I mean, if you want to talk to me, it's fine. I'll do what I can." Then I pause, doubting myself. "If it's something you need Sister for though—"

I'm torn between my intentions and my lack of experience.

"I don't know," she says. "I feel stupid going to her. And then I feel stupid for feeling stupid. It's a vicious circle. I don't want them thinking that I'm incapable or incompetent, you know."

I'm already nodding before she turns to look at me again. I know too well.

"Everyone has been lovely, but I've been trying to do everything, trying to show them that I can do everything. Even though I am new here, and even though they don't know me like they know you."

"That's not necessarily a bad thing," I smile. Her face remains flat, and I drop my grin. "What I mean is, you're new, but they haven't seen you as a student. They don't know anything about what you've experienced during your training. They know you have the skills and competencies to qualify, but beyond that," I shrug, "Well, they don't know much about you at all."

"Sure," she says. "I thought it would be a good idea to appear confident and dive straight in. I can always stop to ask for help if I need to, right?"

"Right," I agree.

"Wrong," she corrects. "Now everyone thinks I can do anything and everything. Whatever comes up, they assume I can take in my stride. I can, pretty much, but when I can't, I don't feel like I can ask for help."

"You can," I interrupt. "You should. What's happened? What do you need help with?"

"I was trying to take blood from one of the babies. The one with jaundice."

I nod, I remember the details from handover.

"Just a simple heel prick, collect the blood in the tube, send it down to the lab."

She frowns as she describes the procedure.

It does sound, simple, if you've never had to do it. Of course, trying to get a few millilitres of blood from a pin prick on a baby's heel isn't always easy at all. Babies wriggle, and don't necessarily lie still for you to manoeuvre their little feet into position. They kick out as you're trying to hold the tiny plastic tube to collect the sample, and sometimes they kick it out of your hand. If you get as far as collecting the blood, that is. Sometimes you do everything you can to gather the blood, and not a single drop comes out. We use a tiny sterile lancet to pierce a baby's skin on the soft fleshy part of their foot, and I've not spoken to anyone yet that doesn't hate having to cause even this pinprick of pain to a newborn.

Nobody takes blood from a baby unless they need to. In this case, when the baby is jaundiced, we need to know how severe the problem is. We need to check the bilirubin levels, see whether they are improving, whether the treatment is working, or whether further action is needed. Beth's patient has been on the BiliBed, receiving phototherapy, a blue spectrum light that helps to break down the bilirubin in the baby's blood. The jaundice is a symptom, the hyperbilirubinemia – the excess bilirubin in the blood – is the actual cause for concern. Too much bilirubin, if left untreated, can lead to serious problems like seizures and even brain damage. Yes, these blood tests are essential.

"It's hard sometimes," I say, gently.

"First time I pricked him, nothing came out. Not a drop. I was stupid enough to let the parents come with the baby to the treatment room. No problem, I thought, I've done this before."

Me, too, but I'm not sure I would be confident enough to be watched. I prefer to explain the procedure and take the baby into the treatment room where I can be comfortable, and where I can concentrate. There's a certain degree of performance anxiety when a parent is watching you carry out a procedure. Heck, I get performance anxiety when another midwife watches me. I was always so nervous as a student when my mentor needed to supervise me doing anything even slightly out of my comfort zone.

"I pricked him again, all apologetic, of course, and feeling awful already. Nothing."

I want to chirp in with some more reassurance, but I let her talk.

"So, I think, maybe I'll try this little trick I learned, you've probably done it too. Get a bowl of warm water, dip his little foot in it for half a minute, get the blood flowing."

I nod. This is one of the things that Geri showed me when she was mentoring me on this ward.

"He didn't seem to mind it at all, sweet little thing. His foot got pink and warm, and when I jabbed him for the third time, he finally let me have some blood."

I crease my brow, wondering how this seemingly straightforward series of events has caused Beth to stand in the storeroom, in her own words, 'hiding'.

"No, it wasn't that easy," she sighs, catching my expression. "He kicked out at the bowl. I hadn't moved it. I was in so much of a rush to get that blood while he was still warm, I didn't want to waste the opportunity and I was in so much of a fluster already. I didn't let it show, of course, I was all calm and cool and 'this is quite normal' with the parents, which it is, right?"

"It is," I say.

"He knocked the water all over the cot, and then the sample bottle slipped out of my hand while I was trying to stop it, and the precious little blood that I had gathered splashed out onto the biliblanket. It looked like a lot more than it actually was, because of the water, and, well, blood always does that, doesn't it? It always looks like more than it is."

"Oh no," I sympathise. She looks exactly as I would look if I had done the same thing. "It's not your fault," I say. "I know, I mean…ugh…" It's hard to console her when my reaction would be identical.

"I wrapped him up in a towel, made my apologies with my best smile and told them I'd get clean sheets and come back. Then I apologised again. And again. And, well, here I am."

"I'm starting to understand," I tell her. "Really, I think I can make sense of what you are feeling."

"And I still have to go back and try it again. He needs that test. I have to get it to the lab."

"You've taken blood from babies before, though," I say. "And you can do it. Sometimes it's more difficult than others." When she doesn't respond, I prompt her. "Right?"

"I feel stupid. I felt so bad in front of the parents, and I feel even worse having to go back. If I fail again…"

"You don't know. You don't know what will happen when you go back." When, not if. I'm not including an option here. "If you need help, you can ask Sam." I pause. "Or me."

Her eyes flicker at the suggestion.

"I'm not saying that I'm any better than you," I say, holding up my hands. "But I'm happy to help, or at least try to."

"Thanks," she says. Taking a deep breath, she repeats the word, with more conviction. "Thanks."

I reach up, take the biliblanket off the shelf and hold it out to her.

"Do you want me to come with you?" I ask. That's better than having me take over, surely. Having me there will either make her feel more confident or more nervous. I don't know her well enough to presume which way it might go, but I feel like I should offer.

She extends a hand and takes hold of the soft blue cloth. I don't let go immediately, and we stand, joined by the cover. Is it an olive branch? I don't know, but the moment feels deeply symbolic. I'm sure I am handing her more than a bed covering.

"Thanks," she says again. Her repetition is neither an acceptance nor a rejection.

I let go of my side of the fabric, and she looks me in the eye, slow and steady before saying for the fourth time. “Thanks. I mean it. I needed this.”

I know she doesn’t mean the biliblanket.

“Don’t mention it,” I say. “Let’s go and take this sample.”

With a determined, more confident smile, she turns and heads for the door, and I follow.

We arrive at the baby’s cot without having spoken another word. When she gets there, she waves the cover at the parents.

“Here we go,” she says. “Let’s get the cot changed and take that sample.” Her voice is so calm, I would never have guessed that she had just been having a mini meltdown unless I knew. “This is Violet,” she says, “One of the other midwives.”

I give the parents a warm, reassuring smile.

The woman is cradling the infant in her arms, smoothing her hand over the sparce covering of hair on his soft head. Neither she, the father nor the child look at all concerned by Beth’s need to change the biliblanket or try again to take the blood sample.

“He’s lovely,” I say. I can see the yellow tinge of jaundice on his skin, but apart from that he looks perfect. There’s something about being at this end of the ward, with a couple and baby that feels like permission to see him as a baby to coo over rather than a patient to care for. Aren’t they all though?

Can't I feel this way about the infants that I'm overseeing? Do I really need a level of detachment just because they are my *patients*? I almost shudder at the word and at the questions I am asking of myself. I'm learning all the time; no matter what I do, I am learning.

I don't know if it's because my calming presence is helping Beth to keep it together, or that she actually is cool and composed, but she preps the area and takes the sample without any trouble at all. The baby doesn't even cry as she gently pierces the fleshy part of his foot with the lancet and collects the blood in the tiny tube.

"All done," she says, with a wide smile, as she passes the baby back to his mother.

She flicks her eyes to me, and I nod. I don't know if I could have come back out here and been as calm as she has been. Perhaps that's the real difference between us. We all get in a flap sometimes, I guess it's all down to how we deal with it.

## Chapter Seventeen

It's after three-thirty when I finally make my way to the locker room to pick up my jacket and bag. It'll be four before I get home, then half an hour to shower and change. Add on the walk to Coffee Express. If I rush, I can probably just about make it on time. My mind is swirling with the thought of whether I should text Zoe and tell her that I am going to be late for our five o'clock meet up when I reach for my bag and almost slam my hand into a figure sitting at the end of the bench.

"Oh gosh I'm sorry. I didn't realise anyone was here."

I'm thankful for the dim lighting because I'm almost certain that my face has turned a bright shade of red.

It's Beth, hunched over something on her lap. I don't catch onto what it is, but she hurriedly tries to cover it up, scrabbling furtively on the floor.

"Uh, it's okay," she breathes, pulling her bag up onto the bench and stashing away whatever it was she was doing.

"I thought everyone had gone home. I—" As she turns back away from her satchel, I see that the confident, calm face that I am used to seeing has been replaced by an expression of sadness. "I was just—" I'm lost for words.

"No, no, it's fine." Beth starts to stand, but I park myself on the bench next to her and press my hand against her arm.

"What is it?" I ask.

She shakes her head, but lets me bring her back down to her seat, flopping firmly into position beside me.

"What were you doing?"

Her head drops forward towards her knees in a forlorn nod and she sits there for a moment, like someone trying to stave off a bout of dizziness. I give her time and sit, letting all my questions bubble in my mind.

Eventually, she whoops in a heavy inhalation and sits upright again, turning to look at me.

"I don't like to take any of it home with me," she says.

At first I don't understand. "Take what home?" I ask. "Is this about what happened earlier."

She nods slowly. "My issues, I guess," she says. "My fears, my problems, my insecurities. You know everyone here. You trained here. Everybody is so supportive and lovely to you. From day one I was left to get on with it, like they didn't even realise that I was newly qualified. I suppose some of them didn't know…and then I felt too stupid to keep telling people. You know?"

"I –"

She continues before I can say anything.

"I don't know anyone. Not just here, I mean I don't know anyone in town. I go home and I'm on my own until I come back here again."

"I didn't realise," I say, but if I had thought about it of course I would have. I didn't think about it, that's the truth.

"No, why should you?" she says. "I've been trying to get on with it, trying to fit in, but when you're starting out somewhere new, doing something as challenging as this, it's tough, isn't it?"

Again, I'm about to answer her and she carries on talking.

"I write it all down. That's what I was doing. I'm usually the last person here. No one notices, not really. You finish your shift and you dash off for your bus or take the car home to your family, friends, whatever. I sit here and offload into my journal." She nods towards the bag on the other side of her.

"Offload?" I repeat the key word.

"The things I've done wrong, the things I need to learn more about, the things I need to do better." Beth reaches back into her bag and pulls out the thick book that she must have been writing in when I entered the room.

"Here," she says. "Look. This is how I cope."

I've never seen her like this before. She seemed unbreakable, but now she is showing the cracks, the cracks that we all have, the cracks that show we are human.

I wave my hand in refusal.

"It's private," I say. "That's your book. They are your thoughts and feelings."

She flashes me a look and opens the dark blue book and starts to read.

"Tuesday. Sabrina Fisher. Blood transfusion. Terrified that I was going to mess up. Felt like I was going to misread the label on the bag or misread her name band. Was the blood too cold? Had I warmed it up too long? Was I doing the right checks? Was I checking up on her too often? Did she think I was clueless?"

"Stop," I tell her, my voice soft and calm. "Beth. Don't."

"But there's more. There's so much more."

I have been so blind to what has been going on around me. I assumed that because Beth looked like she had everything under control that she really had. I never once stopped to think about how she might be feeling. I took everything at face value. My intuition is usually spot on, but maybe it only works for the women in my care, and maybe it fails me when it comes to caring about my colleagues. They have all been there for me. Even Beth has been there for me, despite her personal struggles.

"I'm so sorry," I say. I pause, only for a split second, before reaching my arms out towards her. "I'm sorry, Beth."

She leans forward into the hug and rests her head onto my shoulder.

"I should have realised," I say in a quiet, soothing tone. "I was so wrapped up in my own problems that I forgot that I'm not alone."

"You're an amazing midwife," Beth murmurs against me. "The women love you."

I let out a tiny laugh of disbelief. "No one has ever called me that before, and I'm not sure that I deserve it," I say. "I'm far from amazing."

"You make everyone feel so…I don't know what the word is. I suppose I mean that you make everyone feel important. It never looks as though you are only doing your job. You treat everyone with care and compassion and…Violet, I'm so jealous. I wish I could be more like you."

I draw back so that I can see her face, and she lifts her gaze to meet mine.

"I feel silly now," she smiles.

"No," I say. "Don't. Don't feel silly. What's silly is that I was jealous of you. I saw you breezing through every shift, being brilliant despite being just as new as I am."

It's her turn to laugh. She snorts and covers her mouth with her hand and shakes her head.

"No way," she says. "It's so tough. This book keeps me sane; I swear."

I reach down, take it from her, and leaf through a few pages, skim reading her entries.

"The things that you worry about are the same things that play on my mind too. There's so much to take in, so many new skills to learn, or to remember from when we were following someone else around while we were training. Of course, we aren't going to know everything, there's no way we possibly could."

I don't think I realised that the last sentence was true until I spoke the words aloud, and I sit in stunned silence, looking at my colleague.

"Thank you, Violet," she says. "I think I needed to hear that."

"I think I needed to say it," I reply.

The locker room door clicks open, and one of the domestic assistants walks in.

"Sorry, love. I didn't know you were…"

She turns and shuffles out, just as quickly as she arrived. I look at Beth and shrug.

"Okay then," she smiles.

"Look, let's talk more in future," I say. "Not like this, not scrunched up in the locker room with the late shift's coats dangling over us. Let's make time to catch up and go over some of the things that are on our minds."

Beth agrees. "That would be great. I would like to do that. Very much."

"I have to leave now. I'm meeting my friend for coffee and I need to get home and change first."

Her face falls, and she tries to cover it up, but she's not quick enough for it not to be noticeable.

"If you want," I say, thinking on my feet. "You could come with me? I mean go home and change and then come and meet us?"

"Really?" she asks, her face brightening. "I wouldn't want to be in the way," she says.

"Zoe is the sweetest," I tell her. "She would love to meet you. Don't take this the wrong way, but I have mentioned you in the past." I wish I had kept my mouth shut, because the words sound so stupid, or make me sound stupid.

"I hope it was only good things," she grins.

I take a gulp of air and bite the bullet.

"Beth, I have been an idiot. I've been struggling so hard to fit in and make the change to being a qualified midwife that I've lost sight of what matters. I wanted to be a midwife so that I could help other people, and so that I could support women. When I met you—" I have to stop to think my words out. "You were everything that I wanted to be, and I felt so incompetent compared to you."

"No, Violet," she says, but I stop her.

"I've realised now though. We aren't in competition. There's not a trophy for who gives the best breastfeeding support or does the drugs round in the fastest time."

"Maybe there should be," she jokes.

"Well, maybe, yes. But what I mean is that we all want the same thing. You, me, the other midwives. We are all here to support women, and we should be supporting each other."

She nods silently.

"I'm sorry that I was genuinely jealous of you. And I am sorry that I let you down."

"New start," Beth says.

She extends her hand; I take it and shake it gently.

As we let go, I feel a sweeping wave of relief rush through me.

"Like a weight has been lifted, isn't it?" she says, clearly feeling the change in energy between us too.

"Let me give you my number," I tell her, pulling my phone out of my pocket. "We're meeting at Coffee Express in town at five. Come down. And message me any time, okay?"

Beth grabs her phone too, and we tap each other's details into our contacts.

"Great," she says. "I will. And Violet."

"Yes?"

"You too."

I'm never good at opening up and talking about my problems, but knowing that Beth is going through the same issues as I am somehow makes me feel safe.

We are the only two newly qualified midwives at St. Jude's, of course we need to support each other. It's what midwives do.

# Chapter Eighteen

"So, the catering is all confirmed. Luke agreed to go with the beef after all, and…"

Zoe is mid-way through telling me the latest wedding news when Beth walks into Coffee Express.

"Here she is," I interrupt her with a nudge.

"Ooh," Zoe says.

Mate dates have always been about Zoe and I spending time together, catching up and chilling out, so today's plus one is quite a novelty.

"You're right, she is pretty," Zoe whispers.

"Beth, here!" I call over to her, although as we are sitting in a direct beeline from the entrance it wouldn't have taken her long to see us.

Beth strides over with that confidence that I am used to seeing from her and stands by our table.

"Hi," she smiles. "You must be Zoe."

It's hard to believe that the girl in front of me, the persona that I see on the ward, the smiling, cheerful woman is the same person I sat with in the locker room. She let her vulnerable side show through. I realise that showing fragility takes a level of trust in someone. I should know, after all I have been through.

"This is Beth." I make the redundant introduction as Zoe semi-stands to shake hands with our new friend.

"Let me get you a drink," Zoe says. "And will you have cake? They have some amazing options here. The coffee cake is to die for, but Violet swears by the Bakewell."

And she's off. Where I flounder trying to think of conversation topics, or even choose words that don't make me sound stupid, Zoe says whatever comes into her head. I love her all the more for how different she is from me in that respect.

"Will you have another slice?" Zoe asks me.

"No way," I laugh. "I have a bridesmaid's dress to fit into!"

There's another of our major differences. Zoe could eat an entire Victoria sponge and not put on an ounce. I can look at an almond and gain a stone.

Beth's eyebrows give a flicker of interest at my mention of nuptials, and Zoe is already showing her the diamond band on her finger as the two of them walk over to the counter.

I may have been jealous of Beth's midwifery skills and ease of conversation, but I could never be jealous of the way that Zoe manages to effortlessly click with new acquaintances. She is my best friend, and I can't imagine anything ever coming between us. It's so easy for me to feel insecure on the ward, but my friendship with Zoe is solid, stable, and never under question.

They return with drinks and Beth displays her chunk of Bakewell as she settles into her seat.

"Don't let me stop you talking about your wedding plans," Beth smiles.

"I feel like everyone else in the world is probably bored to tears with my plans," Zoe says. "Violet suffers through endless photographs, Pinterest boards and pages that I pull out of Brides Monthly magazine. I'm sure she will be thrilled that I have someone else to waffle on at."

"Well, I don't expect I'll be thinking about my own plans for a long time yet." Beth draws out the word *long* in dramatic exaggeration.

"Tell me about it," I sigh. "The closest I have to a relationship is a little spider plant I bought for my new place, and I swear it's already looking touch and go between us."

"I had a cat," Beth says. "But he started going to the next-door neighbours' for his dinner, and now I never see him anymore. A cat. I can't even keep a cat happy."

Zoe shakes her head. "Cats are notoriously fickle," she laughs. "You can't take it personally."

"At least it wasn't your boyfriend going next door for his, well, anything," I smile.

"Men, cats, plants. All the same." Beth takes a bite of her cake.

I can't believe that I ever had any negative thoughts about her. In many ways, she's a lot like I am. Even though she is way more confident, despite her doubts, I can see now as she slurps at her coffee and wipes crumbs off her face with the back of her hand, that she is only human. We are all only human, and we all have our doubts and fears. We have to be there for each other. All we can do is support each other as women, as colleagues and as friends.

I'm not sure that I would want Beth to come along to my mate date every week, I do still need my time with Zoe, but I am starting to think we could definitely get along.

I listen to the pair of them chatting. Zoe gets to tell Beth all about the wedding, everything I already know, but now I get to see her talk about it again, as an observer, watching the excitement on her face as she goes over the details. Time is so important to the women I care for on the ward, but time with my best friend is important to me too. Maybe the most important thing in the world. Within a couple of months she will be married, and although I know that our mate dates will continue, I also know that things will most definitely change.

Everything changes.

I left home to go to university, I moved into my own flat, started my new job, and now it looks like I have found a new friend. I've seen Zoe grow from a child to a teenager to a young adult, and I've taken that journey with her. Although we are taking different paths, we are still walking side by side. She may have Luke's hand in hers now, but I know that any time I need her I can reach out and she will be right there, just as I will for her.

Change means breaking away from what we know, from the safe and the familiar, and finding a way to adjust to the new and uncertain. Change is like opening a door and walking through to the countless possibilities that lie behind. Change is finding the courage to pedal our bikes without someone's hand to steady us, but knowing if we need that support it will be right there.

I can't fear change. I can't back away from the challenge of the new because this career, this life that I worked so hard to have is all that I have ever wanted. I have to go forwards, knowing that wherever I walk, and wherever my journey takes me, I am not alone.

I look on, and I smile. My best friend. My new friend. No matter what changes may come, I am not alone.

Dear Reader,

Thank you for reading **"Starting Out"**. Violet and Zoe's stories are not over yet, so keep your eye out for forthcoming releases.

Please sign up to my mailing list to keep up to date with new releases and special offers. I'm currently giving away a free full-length novel to everyone who joins me. Visit **jerowney.com** for details.

If you have enjoyed this book, please consider leaving a review on Amazon and/or Goodreads. Reviews help readers to discover books, and help authors to find new readers. It would mean a lot to me if you would take a few minutes to leave a review.

If you would like to read more about Violet and Zoe, be sure to check out the Lessons of a Student Midwife series.

You can also find me on social media as @jerowneywriter.

See you there!
J.E. Rowney